As Jimmy tore into the lollipop wrapper, Brandon leaned toward her, close enough for her to catch a whiff of his mountain-fresh cologne laced with a manly soap, and said, "I have to admit that the twins' nicknames for you seem suitable."

"How's that?"

"Doughnuts and Lollipops are both sweet."

Coming from anyone else, she might have found that line to be sappy or cheesy—or both. But the way Brandon said it, the way he looked at her with sincerity and attraction dancing in his eyes, it touched her in an unexpected way, causing her cheeks to warm and her heart to flutter.

"Thanks for being so nice to my kids." Appreciation glistened in his eyes—something else, too. But she didn't dare make any assumptions. "We'll see you around."

Marissa sure hoped so. Because Brandon seemed like a sweet guy, too. The kind a woman who'd had her hopes and trust shattered could count on.

* * *

RANCHO ESPERANZA: Never lose hope for love

Dear Reader,

Welcome to Rancho Esperanza, a once-struggling ranch near the fictitious town of Fairborn, Montana. With its quaint shops and tree-lined streets, Fairborn is home to a variety of colorful characters. Whether this is your first visit or your third to the community I created, I hope you'll enjoy your time here.

While I'm writing this letter, 2020 is winding down, and the holidays will soon be here. Family gatherings will be small. Writing this book for you has helped me to escape from the realities we've had to face these past months—the struggles, losses and heartaches.

In *Starting Over with the Sheriff*, you'll meet Deputy Sheriff Brandon Dodd, a single dad who has raised his four-year-old twins since they were babies. Brandon adores the little boy and girl who keep him hopping, and he appreciates the help his aunt and uncle, the owners of the Tip Top Market, have provided him. Recently, he's fallen for Marissa Garcia, a beautiful newcomer in town. Marissa admires the handsome single father, too. That is, until she learns he's a lawman.

Once convicted of a crime she didn't commit, Marissa has spent time behind bars. As a result, she's leery of anyone involved in law enforcement.

I hope you'll enjoy an escape to Fairborn, just as I did. And I hope and pray 2021 brings you peace, love and good health.

Happy reading!

Judy

PS: I love hearing from my readers. You can contact me through my website, judyduarte.com, or on Facebook, Facebook.com/judyduartenovelist. And, if you're a fan of Western romances, check out Wild for Westerns from Harlequin, a Facebook page where many of my Harlequin author friends hang out: Facebook.com/groups/290667098916318.

Starting Over with the Sheriff

JUDY DUARTE

HARLEQUIN

SPECIAL
EDITION

Recycling programs for this product may not exist in your area.

ISBN-13: 978-1-335-40490-9

Starting Over with the Sheriff

Copyright © 2021 by Judy Duarte

This edition published by arrangement with Harlequin Books S.A.

For questions and comments about the quality of this book, please contact us at CustomerService@Harlequin.com.

Harlequin Enterprises ULC
22 Adelaide St. West, 40th Floor
Toronto, Ontario M5H 4E3, Canada
www.Harlequin.com

Printed in U.S.A.

Since 2002, *USA TODAY* bestselling author **Judy Duarte** has written over forty books for Harlequin Special Edition, earned two RITA® Award nominations, won two Maggie Awards and received a National Readers' Choice Award. When she's not cooped up in her writing cave, she enjoys traveling with her husband and spending quality time with her grandchildren. You can learn more about Judy and her books on her website, judyduarte.com, or at Facebook.com/judyduartenovelist.

Books by Judy Duarte

Harlequin Special Edition

Rancho Esperanza

Their Night to Remember
A Secret Between Us

Rocking Chair Rodeo

Roping in the Cowgirl
The Bronc Rider's Baby
A Cowboy Family Christmas
The Soldier's Twin Surprise
The Lawman's Convenient Family

The Fortunes of Texas: Rambling Rose

The Mayor's Secret Fortune

The Fortunes of Texas: All Fortune's Children

Wed by Fortune

Visit the Author Profile page
at Harlequin.com for more titles.

To Vickie Maltby,
who has purchased almost every book I've ever
written. Thanks for your love, support and prayers
over the years. I hope you enjoy this story, too!

Chapter One

Marissa Garcia stooped behind the cash register at Darla's Doughnuts, where she'd stashed her purse, reached inside and hunted for her cell phone.

Once she had it in hand, she straightened and sent a quick text message.

Any news yet?

She waited, and with no dots in response, she turned and placed the phone on the counter, next to the coffee maker. Surely she'd hear something soon.

The little bell on the front door jingled as it opened.

An elderly male voice called out, "It sure smells good in here. Makes me wish I could spend the day working with you, Marissa."

She laughed. "I know, right? I hate to leave, even when I'm off the clock."

In his mid-seventies and an army veteran and officer who'd served in two wars, Vietnam and Desert Storm, Carl Matheson was one of Fairborn's most interesting characters and her favorite customer. She offered him a warm smile. "Good morning, Colonel. How's it going?"

"I can't complain." The colonel, his face craggy, his blue eyes bright and his chin bristled, offered her a wink and a grin as he pushed his red walker into the small shop, slowly making his way to the front of the glass case. "I may not be getting around too good these days, but I'm still walking. And I'm on the right side of the grass." He nodded at the walker that held him steady. "And as long as I use my trusty little speedster, I manage to get my daily exercise."

Marissa bit back a chuckle. "Does your doctor know that your fitness routine is a four-block walk that ends at Darla's Doughnuts?"

The colonel scowled and let out a humph. "Oh, for cripe's sake. Doc Clemmons made me give up my Marlboros and Jack Daniel's. I've gotta reward my efforts somehow. Besides, a little sugar and caffeine never hurt anyone."

As Marissa poured a large coffee into a to-go cup, the colonel arched his neck and peered at the door that led to the small kitchen in back. "You running things on your own again today?"

"Yes, I am." This was the third morning Darla had asked her to manage the shop on her own. It was nice to know that her new employer trusted her to handle things while she was away.

"How's Darla's husband doing? Did Fred finally kick that infection?"

"I was just checking for a text. She took him to the doctor this morning, and I was waiting for an update. So far, no word from her."

"That's too bad," the colonel said. "I hope he doesn't end up losing his leg."

That's what had Darla so concerned. "Yeah, me, too." Marissa added, "So what can I get you today, sir?"

He eyed the variety of doughnuts and muffins, then tapped an arthritic finger against the glass case. "Gimme one of those bear claws and a maple bar. To go. And don't try to slip that fat-free creamer on me. I can tell the difference."

He certainly could. Marissa smiled. "I won't make that mistake again." As she added cream and sugar to his coffee, her cell phone rang. She glanced over her shoulder at the display, hoping to see Darla's name and to hear some good news.

Instead, she spotted an unfamiliar number with a San Diego area code.

"You gotta get that, sweetie? Go on, then."

"No. It's just a junk call." She silenced the ringer and let it roll to voice mail.

San Diego? She hadn't lived in Southern California since she was nineteen. And she hadn't been able to leave soon enough. It had taken her fifteen hundred miles, three different rental agreements in as many locales, and numerous temp jobs to end up in a place she could finally call home—Fairborn, Montana, with its quaint streets, colorful characters and small-town charm.

After placing the colonel's order into a bag, she tucked in a couple of napkins and set it next to the register.

"Don't forget the cream and sugar for my coffee," the colonel said.

"I've already added it—just the way you like it." She'd no more than popped on a lid when her cell phone dinged with a text, which had come from the same phone number. Only a portion of the message showed up on the display, just enough to cause her gut to clench.

Marissa? It's Erik…

Her heart dropped to the pit of her stomach. Her fingers trembled, and her grip loosened. She tried to steady the cup with both hands, only to fumble and drop it on the floor, splashing hot coffee everywhere and drenching the top of her once-white sneakers.

Her cheeks burned as if the coffee had splashed onto her face.

"Hey! You okay, hon?"

Marissa tore her gaze from the blasted phone and turned to the colonel, who stood near the register, his craggy brow furrowed in concern.

"Yes," she said. "I'm fine. Sorry. I'm just a little clumsy today, that's all."

"Join the club. Lately, I've been known to trip and drop things, too." The old soldier frowned, and the crease in his forehead deepened. "But you look like you just saw a ghost."

No. Just his text message.

Or a portion of it.

Erik Crowder. Her stepbrother, the jerk.

She hadn't seen or heard from him in years, and she'd hoped to never hear from him again. Hadn't he done enough to screw up her life? What made him think she'd even consider talking to him?

She'd have to block his number.

"Why are you so skittish?" the colonel asked.

"I…uh…" She glanced at the wet floor. What a mess. She threw a couple of hand towels over the spot and stepped on it, using her coffee-soaked foot to wipe the spill. Then she tucked a long strand of dark hair behind her ear and gathered her composure. "I'm just a little distracted this morning. Darla should have checked in by now, so each time my cell phone pings, I jump."

"She probably just got busy. Besides, she trusts you. I know you haven't worked for her very long, but you're the best employee she's had by far. You've always got a smile that makes the coffee and doughnuts taste better."

"Thanks for the vote of confidence. And you're probably right." But Marissa had learned that there were no certainties in this world. Not even when it came to people she'd once considered family. The hurt and humiliation of their final rejection still bore a hole through her heart.

As Marissa filled a replacement cup with the colonel's coffee, her hands continued to tremble, but she pushed through her uneasiness and, this time, securely snapped the lid in place. Then she put the cup in a cardboard carrier meant to hold four and set it and the white bag on the seat of his walker. "There you go. That'll be three dollars and twenty-five cents." She looked up and managed a smile. "The entertainment was on the house."

He chuckled and paid with a five. After she gave him his change, he stuck a dollar in her tip jar then turned toward the door.

"Thanks, Colonel." She walked to the front of

the shop and opened the door for him. "I'll see you tomorrow."

As the sweet old man began his walk home, her mind skipped back to the text message, and her heart continued to pound as if she'd just run a marathon.

Why on earth would Erik contact her? And why now, after all this time, after all he'd done?

Once back behind the counter, she stopped to pick up the rags she'd thrown on the coffee. She started to take them to the sink in back, but curiosity nagged at her until she picked up the cell phone to read the entire text.

Marissa? It's Erik. I need to talk to you. Please call me.

It would be a blustery winter day in hell before she called the guy who'd ruined her life.

And she'd be darned if she'd let Erik's text rent space in her head and ruin her morning. At least, not any more than it already had.

She carried the coffee-soaked towels to the kitchen. Then she grabbed a mop and returned to the front of the shop. She'd barely made a sweep across the floor when her phone dinged again, so she set the mop aside and snatched her cell from the counter.

This time, it *was* Darla who'd sent the text.

Sorry. My sister called this morning, and the time got away from me. How are things going?

Marissa had barely typed out *Okay* when the front door squeaked open and two preschoolers rushed into the shop, breathless and beaming.

"We beated him here," a towheaded little boy said.

"Yeah." The girl, her red curly hair pulled back into a ponytail, nodded. "He's a slowpoker."

Marissa broke into a smile. "Good morning. Who are you two winners racing?"

"Our daddy." The boy walked up to the display case and peered inside. "He said we could run ahead of him. And we did."

"We wanted ice cream," the red-haired girl said. "Aunt Carlene always takes us to Doc Creamer's after we go to the dentist or to the doctor or the appointment with Miss Shirley, but Daddy brung us this time 'cause the ice-cream place is closed right now."

Doc Creamer's Frozen Emporium was a popular place in town, but they didn't open until eleven or later.

"I really wanted a chocolate ice-cream cone," the boy said, "but doughnuts are good, too. Can I have that white one with the little brown candies on top?"

The girl gave him a nudge. "Jimmy, don't be bossy. You forgot to tell her *please*."

"Don't tell me what to do, Maddie. I was just going to say that." Jimmy, a cute little boy with a scatter of freckles across his nose, offered Marissa a smile. "Please can I have that doughnut? And my sister wants a pink one."

"Let's wait until your mommy and daddy get here," Marissa said.

"We don't have a mommy," the girl said. "Only a daddy."

Marissa sucked in a breath. Poor kids.

"But we got two aunties," the boy chimed in. "And they're just as good as two mommies. Huh, Maddie?"

"Yeah." Maddie nodded. "That's what Aunt Betty Sue told us."

"I'm sure she's right," Marissa said. "I don't have a mother, either. But I had an awesome daddy." Not a day went by that she didn't miss him, didn't wish she was still six years old and could crawl up on his lap and listen to his stories—those he read and those he created in his head.

"Our daddy is awesome, too," the girl said, and they exchanged a smile.

Marissa liked children, the younger the better. And she couldn't remember the last time she'd seen two who were cuter than these.

The bell on the door tinkled again, and a handsome, dark-haired man walked in—all buff and hunky. And far more gorgeous than a daddy had a right to be, especially when he shot Marissa a dimpled grin.

Dang. He was a gorgeous doppelgänger of Scott Eastwood, and if she didn't know any better, she'd think there must be a Hollywood film crew in town.

"I hope these little ragamuffins haven't been giving you any trouble," he said.

"Not at all." Marissa returned his smile.

"Now can we get our doughnuts?" Jimmy asked. "Please. And can I have a chocolate milk to drink?"

Maddie—his twin sister, she guessed—chimed in. "Me, too. Please."

Marissa glanced at Mr. Daddy for his okay. When he nodded, she said, "Two doughnuts and chocolate milks coming right up."

After retrieving the children's orders, she shot a smile at Mr. Daddy. "Can I get you something?"

"Coffee. Black." He gave her a quick once-over, then smiled. "You're new in town."

Apparently, he wasn't. And while she'd never offer up much about her past, she couldn't see any reason not to answer a simple question—honestly. "Yes. I moved here last month."

"Where are you from?"

"Originally? San Diego." She didn't need to tell him the roundabout way she'd come here.

"Nice city. Well, welcome to Fairborn."

"Thanks." She cast a glance at his left hand and noted the absence of a ring. So he hadn't remarried, although the kids mentioned not having a mom. Widowed? Divorced?

She glanced at the rest of him. Broad shoulders and bulging biceps suggested that he either had a well-used gym membership or a job that required strength and stamina. Maybe he worked in construction, although he was obviously off this morning.

Before either of them could speak, a thump sounded and the boy shrieked, drawing the adults' attention. Little Jimmy sat on the floor, his doughnut lying next to him—frosting-side down.

"Maddie!" he shouted, tears welling in his eyes. "Look what you made me do!"

"I didn't do anything," his sister said. "You shouldn't have stood on the chair."

Mr. Daddy was at his side in a minute. "You okay, Jimmy?"

"No. My elbow hurts. And now I don't have a doughnut."

Marissa snatched a fresh doughnut from the case—chocolate with white frosting and sprinkles. "You're in luck. I have another one just like it."

Daddy helped the boy get up, took a peek at

his elbow and then set the toppled chair upright. "What'd I tell you about feet belonging on the floor and not on the furniture? There's a good reason for the rules we have. Do you need a time-out to help you to remember?"

"No. I'm sorry."

"Don't do it again," the dad said, kissing the boy's forehead. "And your elbow is fine."

Marissa scooped the remainder of the downed doughnut into her hands and carried it to the trash can. Then she reached for a damp rag and returned to the accident site, where she wiped up all traces of frosting and crumbs.

"I'm sorry that I made your chair fall down," Jimmy said to Marissa.

"No problem, honey. Accidents happen. In fact, I spilled some coffee myself earlier." She pointed the toe of her stained sneaker at him.

They shared a smile.

Seeing her coffee-stained shoe jogged her memory. She looked at the boy's dad. "Speaking of coffee, let me get that for you."

"It's no problem. Thanks so much for your help." He tossed her a heart-strumming grin. "I can take it to go."

So he didn't plan to stay. Not that she'd expected him to, but... Well, she'd kind of like to get to know him and the kids a little better.

She filled his cup with coffee. "Cream and sugar?"

"No, thanks. Black." He grinned.

"Oh, right. You said that before. You got it." Now she sounded like a dingbat. Way to make a good impression… *Not.*

After handing him his coffee, she rang up the tab. "That'll be seven dollars and fifty cents."

He pulled a wallet from his hip pocket and withdrew a ten. "Here you go. Keep the change."

"You don't have to…" She caught herself. Not everyone who dangled money in front of her expected a favor, one that might backfire and give her a ton of grief.

"I know I don't need to. But—" he winked "—consider it a cleaning deposit. We'll be back, and who knows what'll happen next." Then he gathered up the kiddos and lovingly guided them out of the shop.

He took one last look over his shoulder at her and tossed her a smile before he shut the door behind him. He'd made a point of saying he'd come back. She certainly hoped it would be on a Tuesday or Thursday, the only mornings she worked here—unless Darla needed her.

It would be nice if he brought the kids with him. Whenever she saw a father who appeared to be devoted to his children, like her dad had been to her, it warmed her heart and sparked memories of the short time she'd had with him.

She'd never known her mom, but her dad had raised her until she was twelve. If the gentle giant hadn't died, her life, especially her teen years, would've been so much better.

Yet it was more than Mr. Daddy's paternal side that caused her heartbeat to kick its pace up a notch. It was his manly brawn and the dazzling pair of baby blues that made her feel like a woman in need of...

Well, she certainly didn't *need* a man in her life. She'd learned long ago not to rely on anyone other than herself. But it would be nice to get to know him better. And maybe even go out...

Oh, for Pete's sake. Her thoughts were spiraling. She'd have to put the whole dating thing on the back burner, especially when it came to Mr. Daddy.

Not that the kids were a problem. It was his marital status. Or lack of. Even if his wife had died, there had to be others on her side of the family, people ready to judge an outsider. And any sign of potential trouble like that would be a real game changer.

She knew that from experience.

On the drive to Tip Top Market, where Brandon Dodd would drop off the kids with his aunt and uncle, he glanced into the rearview mirror, where his four-year-olds were secured in their boosters in the back seat of his new Jeep Grand Cherokee. He always got a kick out of their childhood chatter, especially when they didn't know he was eavesdropping. Their take on life never ceased to amaze him.

"I like her," Maddie said. "Don't you, Jimmy?"

"Who?" her twin asked, as he held a red-caped superhero toy and zoomed it through the air.

"The doughnut lady. She smells good. Like Miss Cynthia at preschool."

"Yeah. She's nice. Nicer than Miss Cynthia. Because she didn't get mad at me when my chair fell down. At school, when it happened, I had to sit in time-out."

"I know," Maddie said. "And that nice lady gave you a free doughnut, too."

"Yep."

Brandon grinned. He liked the doughnut lady, too. And not just because she was attractive. He especially liked the fact that she'd been sweet and kind to the twins. He might be biased, but they were awesome kids—Jimmy with his scruffy, dusty-blond hair that seemed to have a mind of its own. That is, until Brandon helped him wet it down each morning. And Maddie, with her red curls that were just as wild. Fortunately, Brandon had learned to tame them using ribbons and barrettes—thanks to the help of the preschool director, who had noticed her crazy hair and given him some hands-on help. He wasn't a natural, but for a single dad? His hairdressing skills were improving.

He smiled again at Jimmy and Maddie. Sure, they could both be naughty sometimes, but hey. What kids weren't?

His mood darkened. He wondered if their mother ever thought about them, if she ever felt the least bit guilty about giving them up so easily.

Probably not. But her loss was his gain. He had no idea what his life would be like without them.

"Daddy," Maddie said, "what's the doughnut lady's name?"

"I don't know, honey." Brandon should have asked her when he'd had the chance, and while loading the kids into their booster seats, he'd kicked himself for leaving without doing so. But it'd be easy enough to find out. "I agree with you, honey. She was very nice."

"She's pretty like a princess," Maddie added, as she ran a pink toy comb through her dolly's curls, catching a snag.

No argument there. With long wavy dark hair and warm brown eyes, the doughnut lady didn't need a tiara or a gown to draw a man's attention. And the fact that she seemed to have a way with kids was a plus. Not that he planned to introduce a woman into their lives yet—much to the chagrin of his great-aunt, Betty Sue.

You're too young and good-looking to be single, Betty Sue had told him time and again. *It isn't natural for a man your age to be celibate.*

Brandon wasn't exactly celibate, although it felt like that sometimes. But he wasn't about to discuss his love life, as rare as it might be, with one of his relatives, especially a woman in her mid-seventies.

"Daddy," Jimmy said, "how come we can't go to the park? It's not a school day."

"That would be fun, sport. But I have an important meeting at lunchtime, so I have to take you back to the market."

Brandon had been depending upon his aunt and uncle to watch the twins since the day he'd packed them both in rear-facing car seats and brought them home from college, along with a bachelor's degree in criminal justice.

Brandon had hated to ask his aunt and uncle, Ralph and Carlene Tipton, to babysit since running the market kept them both busy. But they'd jumped at the chance and were delighted to help out.

When Brandon had been in the seventh grade, his parents had gone through a nasty divorce. They'd barely been able to take care of themselves, let alone provide him with a stable home, so he'd contacted his uncle and told him how he was being left alone for days on end.

While Aunt Carlene watched the market, Uncle Ralph drove most of the night to pick him up. After being confronted about their neglect, Brandon's mom and dad had willingly signed over custody to the Tiptons. Then Ralph took Brandon home with him to live in Fairborn. The way Brandon saw it, they'd saved his life.

You couldn't find two finer people than his aunt and uncle, even though they did get a little too opinionated, especially when it came to his personal life.

"Stop it, Jimmy. You poked me."

"I didn't. Super Dude did it."

Brandon glanced in the rearview mirror. "If Super Dude can't respect his own airspace, I'm going to take him away from you."

Jimmy scowled at his sister. "I don't tell on your princess doll when she pokes me."

Brandon fought the smile that tugged at his lips, then, taking note of his son's scruffy hair, said, "I think it's time for a visit to The Mane Event, Jimmy."

"I don't wanna get my hair cut. How come I always have to go and Maddie doesn't?"

"Because," his sister said, "I keep my hair out of my face with barrettes and ribbons. And you don't."

"That's because I'm a boy."

"I'll tell you what," Brandon said, as he turned into the graveled drive and parked in front of the market. "I don't have to work tomorrow. So we'll get Jimmy's hair cut. And afterward, why don't we stop by Darla's for another doughnut? How does that sound?"

"Good!" Maddie said.

"Can we get the doughnut first?" Jimmy asked. "And then get a haircut?"

"Sorry, son. That's not how rewards work."

"That's how I think it should work," Jimmy muttered.

For a guy who wasn't all that big on sweets, Brandon had a real hankering for a bear claw. Hopefully, the pretty woman who his kids called the doughnut lady would be working tomorrow morning. And he'd learn a little more about her, starting with her name.

Marissa closed up the doughnut shop at two, then she headed back to Rancho Esperanza, where she'd been staying for the past few days. It had been a godsend when Alana Perez offered her room and board if she'd help with the gardening, canning and baking. Marissa needed to build up her savings account, which wasn't growing fast enough for the plans she'd made.

She'd only managed to find part-time positions—one at Darla's and another as a reception-ist at The Mane Event. She had higher hopes for herself than just working for someone else, but for now, it was okay. Plus, on the upside, those two employers hadn't asked for references—or run a background check.

Besides, Alana kept her pretty busy at the ranch. It took a lot of work to get ready for the farmers market on the weekends. And since Callie, who'd lived at the ranch until she married Mayor Ramon Cruz, had moved to town, Alana needed all the help she could get. Besides, she really enjoyed working with her new landlady.

Marissa had just turned onto the county road in the ten-year-old sedan she'd named Prudence when her cell phone rang. Ever since Erik had tried to contact her, she'd been careful about checking to see who might be looking for her. There was no way she'd talk to the guy. Even if he only wanted to explain or apologize for what he'd done, she wouldn't accept it. Not after what he'd put her through.

Fortunately, this call was from Alana. She tapped the speaker icon on the screen.

"Hey," Marissa said. "What's up?"

"Are you still in town?"

"No. I'm about ten minutes away from the ranch. Why?"

"Because I'm elbows-deep in bread dough for

the cinnamon rolls I'm making. I thought they might go over well at the farmers market and wanted to try the recipe first. But I just realized I'm out of powdered sugar."

"I'll turn around," Marissa said.

"No, you don't need to do that. Just stop at Tip Top Market. It's only about a mile down the road from here."

"Do you need anything else while I'm there?"

"Not that I can think of. But then again, I can't believe how forgetful I've been lately. I think the hormones have made my brain go wonky."

A smile tugged at Marissa's lips. "I've heard pregnancy will do that to you."

"It's a little annoying, but I'm so glad to be pregnant I don't care."

"And just think. You'll have a baby boy in a few short months."

"I think about that all the time. So I'm even grateful for all the little annoyances."

Alana and her fiancé, Clay Hastings, were looking forward to getting married next month, and they'd agreed to let Marissa plan their wedding. If everything went according to plan, and Marissa was able to build up her meager savings, she'd eventually be able to give notice to her employers and launch a brand-new career as a wedding planner. She even had a name for it: White Lace and Promises.

When she spotted the Tip Top Market and Casino sign up ahead, she pulled into the graveled driveway and parked near the front door. It didn't look like there were too many customers, so she ought to be in and out quickly.

She reached for her purse, locked the car door and headed inside.

Marissa had met Carlene Tipton at Callie's baby shower, but she hadn't stopped at the market before today. She'd passed this place several times and was curious about it.

Once inside, she scanned the interior. The market carried all the basics, including snacks and canned goods. It also boasted a pair of slot machines that sat to the right of the checkstand. Country music played on a radio behind a glass-front counter.

"Hey!" A little girl's voice rang out. "Jimmy, look who's here! The doughnut lady!"

"Uh-oh. Oops!"

Before Marissa could turn around, pain exploded in her forehead.

Chapter Two

Marissa gasped, rubbing her forehead and glancing around for the object that had narrowly missed her eye. There, down on the green tile floor, lay a little action figure wearing a red cape, its head dangling to the side.

"Jimmy!" the girl called out. "You're gonna get in trouble. I'm telling Uncle Ralph you hit a customer."

Tears welled in the boy's eyes. "I didn't mean to."

Marissa again touched her forehead, which still stung from the impact, then she stooped to pick up the plastic toy and made her way to where Jimmy stood. "I think this belongs to you."

"I'm sorry, Doughnut Lady." The boy bit down on his bottom lip, then took the toy from her. He looked at the wobbly head, which listed to the side. "Oh, no. And I killed Super Dude."

"It looks like he and I were both injured in a midair collision," Marissa said. "Accidents happen, right?"

At that, an elderly woman wearing a lime-green scarf as a headband approached. It was Betty Lou—no, that wasn't right. It was Betty Sue.

She raised her finger, the nail painted a bright red, and pointed it at the boy. "Jimmy, what did we tell you about throwing things indoors? You have a playroom in the back of the store. It looks like you need to spend a little thinking time in the corner." Then she turned to Marissa and sighed. "I'm sorry about that. I'm afraid my nephew is a little impulsive at times. Probably takes after me."

"No harm done," Marissa said.

A bright smile lit Betty Sue's blue eyes and softened the lines on her face. "Hey. I know you. We met at Callie's baby shower."

"Yes, we did." Marissa wasn't surprised to see Betty Sue at the market. After all, she lived with the Tiptons, who were the owners. But she hadn't expected to see the twins here. Was their daddy here, too?

"You're the doughnut lady," Maddie said, as

she turned to Betty Sue. "Isn't she pretty? Daddy thinks so, too."

Betty Sue brightened. "You don't say. I always knew that man had good taste. And a good eye."

"He's gotta have good eyes," Jimmy said. "And he's gotta be strong and a fast runner. That's why he goes to the gym."

"Yeah," Maddie said. "He's a hero."

"That he is, sweet pea." Betty Sue placed a hand on Jimmy's shoulder. "Uncle Ralph is a whiz at fixing things. If you take Super Dude to him, I'll bet he'll have his head upright in no time at all."

"Okay. Come on, Maddie."

As the children headed to the back of the market, Betty Sue leaned toward Marissa, cupped her hand around her mouth and lowered her voice. "Their father is a hero, but the most heroic thing he's ever done was to take responsibility of two babies, twins not even a year old. And for a man who grew up as an only child, he's done an amazing job of it. 'Course, Brandon's got me, Ralph and Carlene to help out."

"Hello, there." An older man wearing a green shopkeeper's apron approached the register with a broom, the twins tagging along behind him. "I'm sorry about the...um...mishap. Jimmy means well."

"Mr. Tipton?" Marissa asked.

"Yes, that's me."

"It's nice to meet you." She held out a hand to greet him. "I'm Marissa Garcia. I'm living with Alana at Rancho Esperanza."

"And she's the doughnut lady I told you about," Maddie added. "Doesn't she look like a princess?"

Marissa flushed. "I don't know about that." Other than her father, no one else had ever thought she had a drop of royal blood, although it was sweet that Maddie did.

"Can I help you find something?" Mr. Tipton asked.

Yes, she thought. *Where is the children's father?* Instead, she said, "I stopped to buy powdered sugar."

"It's in aisle three."

Marissa nodded. "Thank you."

"Ralph," Betty Sue said, "you can go back to what you were doing—and supervising Jimmy's time-out. I'll man the cash register for you. It'll give me time to get to know our new neighbor a little better."

Marissa would like to quiz Betty Sue further, too, but she'd better be subtle. She didn't want anyone to suspect she was curious about the heroic single daddy. At least she'd learned something.

His name was Brandon. And it would seem that his wife, the twins' mother, had died. Or else she was unfit for one reason or another. Ei-

ther way, the mom and her family weren't helping very much—if at all. So, if that was the case,
maybe she shouldn't write off the single daddy
completely.

Brandon had barely stepped foot into the Tip
Top Market to pick up the kids when Betty Sue
jumped up from her seat in front of her favorite
slot machine, nearly knocking over the stool. Then
she hurried toward him, while adjusting the green
scarf she used to hold her red curls in place.

"Slow down," he said. "I don't want you falling and screwing up your knee again."

"I'm just as steady on my feet as ever. Don't
worry about me. Besides, Ralph sold the motor-
cycle, remember?"

After she'd taken off on the bike, she'd spun
out in the gravel and wrenched her right knee.

"Oh, that Ralph." Betty Sue huffed. "It was just
an accident. I was perfectly fine driving around
that red hot mama."

Brandon grinned. "Ralph was only looking out
for you."

"And I'm looking out for you." She pointed a
finger at him and burst into a bright-eyed grin.
"I've got some news you need to hear."

Brandon wasn't so sure about that. His great-
aunt always seemed to have wild ideas.

"What's up?" he asked, hoping her so-called

news didn't have anything to do with Jimmy and Maddie.

"We had a visitor this afternoon."

"Oh, yeah?" Brandon scanned the market, looking for the twins.

"Her name is Marissa Garcia. And I can give you the 4-1-1 on her."

"Who?" He wasn't following her. But then again, it wasn't always easy to tune in to his great-aunt's wavelength.

"Marissa. The kids call her the doughnut lady. The pretty princess who works at Darla's Doughnuts."

At that, Brandon tuned right in. "How do you know her?"

"I met her at Callie's baby shower. And then I saw her again today when she stopped in to buy powdered sugar. The kids told me they like her. And that you do, too."

He'd liked her, all right. He'd also felt a hormonal rush he hadn't had since the kids' mother had left him three years ago. "She was nice to the twins. And she didn't blink an eye when Jimmy knocked over his chair."

"I'm not surprised." Betty Sue chuckled. "She was fairly calm this afternoon when Jimmy launched Super Dude across three aisles and accidentally nailed her in the head."

"Oh, no. Was she hurt?"

"Nope. Just a little bump on the noggin. Unfortunately, I can't say the same for Super Dude, who lost his head." Betty Sue laughed, her eyes sparkling with mirth. "Anyway, Marissa is twenty-five. She's originally from San Diego, but we're in luck. She plans to stay in Fairborn."

Interesting, he thought. But he kept his facial expression in check. Betty Sue didn't need any encouragement. She was a romantic at heart, which was a little surprising since she'd never been married.

"Just so you know," Betty Sue added, "Marissa works at the doughnut store a couple days a week. Usually on Tuesdays and Thursdays. She's also answering phones at that new hair salon on Wednesdays and Fridays."

How about that? Brandon's plan to get Jimmy a haircut had moved up on his priority list, although he kept that to himself, too.

"And speaking of hair salons, you really ought to make an appointment with someone there at The Mane Event. They'll do a much nicer job than the barber you see in Kalispell." Betty Sue clucked her tongue. "Why you men favor those short military cuts is beyond me. Most women like it long. That's why Jason Momoa is so popular. Talk about a gorgeous hunk. Every one of my friends on social media drool over him."

"I don't think I'd like to have women drooling over me."

"Oh, come on. They already do. In case you didn't notice, you're considered one of Fairborn's most eligible bachelors."

He'd noticed. And up until now, he hadn't given his so-called eligibility much thought.

"Marissa is also taking a business class at the junior college," Betty Sue added.

"She is?" He picked up a copy of the local paper that was sitting on the counter and pretended to scan the front page.

"Up until last weekend, she was living in a studio apartment in town, but she just moved to the Lazy M, which is going through a renovation of some kind."

Brandon knew the place well. Jack McGee had owned it, and right before he passed, he'd changed his will and left it to Alana Perez, the granddaughter he hadn't known he'd had. The women who lived there referred to it as Rancho Esperanza these days, although the folks in town hadn't gotten used to the name change yet.

"You haven't asked me if Marissa is single," Betty Sue added, "but I've got the scoop on that. She's not even dating anyone, but that's not going to last for very long. So if you've got your eye on her, you'd better make a move. And a quick one."

Brandon laughed off the comment, but Betty

Sue was right on all counts. He *was* interested in Marissa. But was he up to dating anyone right now?

Ever since he'd moved back to Fairborn toting a baby carrier in each hand, he'd been dragging his feet about doing any serious dating. Life was complicated enough running around after the twins. At least, that had always been his default excuse. His smile faded as he thought back to the day Julie had stood in the hallway of the small on-campus apartment they'd shared, a suitcase in hand.

I'm sorry, she'd said. *I didn't mean for this to happen. But he's...my soul mate.*

What am I? Besides stupid, he'd thought.

She flicked a strand of long blond hair behind her shoulder and blew out a weary sigh. *I didn't think you'd understand.*

Brandon had held his hands at his side, fists clenched, keeping his mouth shut and his temper in check. He'd known Julie had once been involved with a guy who'd landed in prison. But he hadn't expected her to hook up with him after he was paroled. *What about the babies?*

This is your night to watch them. So I'll come back for them later.

The hell she would. *I'm the one they've bonded with. You've been too damned busy to be a mother.*

I'll call you after I get settled.

For the next couple of weeks, they'd shared

baby duties, although he'd kept the twins most of the time since she'd always had one excuse or another for changing the plan. On the days leading up to graduation, he'd finally asked her what it would take for her to sign over full custody to him.

She seemed to think about it for the longest time. *I have student loans that'll take time to pay off...*

Done. I'll have the papers drawn up.

He'd had to go to his aunt and uncle for help—mostly with childcare. But he'd paid the cost. Every dime.

And he'd never heard from her again.

Back then, Brandon had been hurt and angry, but his feelings for Julie had dissipated with time and distance. Any residual resentment he held now was on Jimmy and Maddie's behalf. It killed him to think that their mother had abandoned them, like his parents had done to him.

But hey. Live and learn. Besides, he was smart enough to know that not all women were alike. And up until now, he simply hadn't had the time or the desire to date again—at least, not when it came to pursuing a serious relationship with someone in particular.

"So...?" Betty Sue said. "What are you going to do about Marissa?"

Brandon bent and placed a kiss on his great-aunt's brow. "Thanks for the report. I'll give it some thought."

But he wouldn't be thinking too long.

Marissa didn't mind handling the phones and setting appointments at the salon. The additional work would help her build up her savings account. And thanks to Alana's friendship and her offer of room and board in lieu of work on Rancho Esperanza, Marissa no longer had to set aside the funds for rent, which meant that she'd able to move forward on her business plan to start White Lace and Promises sooner than she'd once hoped.

When the telephone rang, Marissa answered in a chipper voice, one that came naturally on such a nice Montana blue-sky day. "The Mane Event. How may I help you?"

"This is Marianne Posey. I'd like to make an appointment on Saturday with Hailey. Does she have time for a touch-up and a trim?"

"Possibly. Let me check." Saturdays were always busy at the salon, but Marissa might be able to find a time for Marianne. Hailey, who looked like she could be Taylor Swift's younger sister, was one of the newest hairstylists Tameka Miller, the owner, had hired. Fresh out of beauty school, Hailey was still trying to build up her clientele.

"Can you come in at three o'clock?" Marissa asked.

"Yes, I can. That'll work perfectly. Thank you."

She'd no more than ended the call and penciled in Marianne Posey's name when the salon door opened. Marissa glanced up to see Mr. Daddy, otherwise known as Brandon, walk in looking like a dream come true—a six-foot-tall hunk, with green eyes and neatly trimmed light brown hair. He certainly didn't need an appointment, but he had little Jimmy in tow.

"Good morning," she said with a smile. "What a surprise." And a very nice one.

He tossed a boyish grin right back at her, setting her heart strumming and knocking her a little off stride.

"Jimmy needs a haircut," Brandon said. "Is there any chance we can get it done today?"

Marissa double-checked with the salon's second-newest stylist, hired just a week before Hailey. "You're in luck." Marissa said. "Robin's available now."

"Does she give lollipops to good kids?" Jimmy asked. "The barber that Uncle Ralph takes me to does."

"Actually," Marissa said, "I'm the one who passes out the candy at this salon. I even have dog treats."

The little towhead's big blue peepers widened. "Do dogs get their haircuts here, too?"

"No, but they sometimes come in with their

owners, although they have to wait outside for them. And if they're good and wait patiently on their leashes, they get a treat, too."

As Robin approached the front of the salon, Marissa tossed a grin at Jimmy and winked. "Should I tell her to duck in case there are any superheroes flying through the air?"

"Nope. I don't even have a toy with me." Jimmy's expression sobered, and he bit down on his bottom lip.

Brandon gave him a little nudge. "Don't you have something to say to Marissa?"

The boy nodded. "I'm sorry that I hit you with my toy yesterday."

"It only hurt for a minute." She pointed to her forehead and showed him the redness hadn't lasted. "See? All better."

"Yep." Jimmy looked up at his father. "I told you she didn't get hurt too bad."

"That's not the point, son. I hope that time-out Uncle Ralph gave you will help you remember not to throw things indoors, especially in the market. And to be more careful with your toys."

"It did, Daddy."

What a good father, Marissa thought. Teaching his son right from wrong. To be kind. And thoughtful.

"Hey, there," Robin said in her gravelly former-smoker's voice. When she reached the front desk, she greeted Jimmy first, then Brandon. "What're we doing to his hair today, Dad?"

"Just a trim. Nothing fancy."

"You've got it." Robin took Jimmy by the hand. "Come on, sweetie."

Marissa expected Brandon to follow his son to Robin's chair, but he didn't, which pleased her in an unexpected way.

"My aunt told me that you're living at Alana's ranch these days. How are things going?"

"Great. We've been making cherry jam and baking bread. We've been selling produce and baked goods at the farmers market on the weekend."

"How's it going?"

"Great. We usually sell out."

"I'm glad to hear it."

"It keeps us busy. But it's been fun working as a team." Marissa tucked a strand of hair behind her ear. "I'm also helping Alana get ready for her wedding. She and Clay are getting married in a few weeks. On the ranch. And I'm helping them with the details."

"Oh, yeah? Isn't her future husband living in Texas?"

"Not anymore. Clay lives at the ranch now. And he's helping Alana with the repairs. He's also studying for the Montana bar, so he'll be able to open a practice here."

"That's good. Henry Dahlberg just retired, so it will be nice to have a new attorney in town."

"I think so, too." Marissa's eyes brightened, her excitement at planning her very first wedding impossible to hide. "Mr. Hastings, Clay's father, had expected them to get married at a fancy country club in Texas and wanted to pull out all the stops. But Alana and Clay want an outdoor wedding on Rancho Esperanza. And I think that's a perfect choice for them."

"Betty Sue said you'd like to start your own business as a wedding planner, so that sounds like a great project for you."

"Yes, that's true." The conversation flowed easily between them, and Marissa found herself opening up to him. "In fact, if I get off early, which probably won't happen today, I thought about stopping by the Petal Pusher to get some ideas about flowers so I can make suggestions."

"Sounds like it'll be a nice wedding." Brandon studied her for a moment, as if he could see something deep inside her that others were too busy to notice. "It also sounds like you're a true romantic."

"I don't know about that. I'm good at organizing parties and events."

"Does that mean you already have your own wedding all planned out?"

"Oh, no." She lifted her hand, palm-side out as

if to halt that thought. "I mean, maybe. Someday. But I've yet to meet a man I can trust."

Brandon sobered. "That's too bad."

She hadn't meant to use the word *trust*, although it was definitely fitting. But she didn't want to come across as a battered butterfly on its last wing. Even if she *had* been let down again and again. "What I meant to say was I haven't found the right man. And I'm really not looking."

Before Brandon could respond, his cell phone rang. He whipped it out of his pocket and glanced at the display. "I'm sorry," he said. "I have to take this."

"Of course."

Brandon walked outside, where he paced near the front window.

She wondered who'd called him. It sounded important. And he clearly wanted a private conversation.

Before she could give it much thought, the salon phone rang, and she went back to work. Still, she found herself stealing a peek out the window at Brandon every now and then—until he caught her. He grinned, and her cheeks flushed.

What a dingbat. Get a grip, Marissa. Don't let him think you're crushing on him, even if you are.

Five minutes later, Brandon stepped back into the salon, just as Jimmy ran up to the front desk and announced, "I'm all done."

"Don't you look handsome!" Marissa said.

"And she said I was good." Jimmy turned to Robin for validation. "Right?"

"He certainly was."

Brandon handed the stylist a five-dollar tip. "Thanks for squeezing us in."

"No problem. Thanks for letting me cut your little guy's hair."

Marissa reached into the drawer, pulled out a small basket filled with lollipops. She lowered it for Jimmy to see. "Why don't you choose one for you—and one for your sister, too."

He reached for a green one, then, after a little thought, he withdrew a red one. "Thank you." He paused for a moment, then looked up at Marissa and grinned. "You know what? You're really nice."

Marissa returned his smile. "And you're sweet. So is Maddie."

"When I get home, I'm going to tell my sister that you're a doughnut lady *and* a lollipop lady."

"I suppose you can say that," she said. "But you can call me Marissa. That is, if you want to."

"Okay. Can Maddie call you that, too?"

"Of course."

As Jimmy tore into the lollipop wrapper, Brandon leaned toward her, close enough for her to catch a whiff of his mountain-fresh cologne laced with a manly soap, and said, "I have to admit that the twins' nicknames for you seem suitable."

"How's that?"

"Doughnuts and lollipops are both sweet." Coming from anyone else, she might have found that line to be sappy or cheesy—or both. But the way Brandon said it, the way he looked at her with sincerity and attraction dancing in his eyes, touched her in an unexpected way, causing her cheeks to warm and her heart to flutter.

"Thanks for being so nice to my kids." Appreciation glistened in his eyes—something else, too. But she didn't dare make any assumptions. "We'll see you around."

Marissa sure hoped so. Because Brandon seemed like a sweet guy, too. The kind a woman who'd had her hopes and trust shattered could count on.

Chapter Three

Brandon didn't make rash decisions, but he'd had a few days to consider the best way to ask Marissa out—and where he should take her. His first thought was something simple and safe, like going to Doc Creamer's Frozen Emporium for an ice-cream sundae. But that seemed a little too family-like, the kind of place parents took their kids. He didn't want her to think he was looking for a mother for the twins.

Going to the movies wouldn't give them an opportunity to talk. Plus, The Reel Deal, the dollar theater in Fairborn, might make him look like a cheapskate. So if he went that route, he'd have to take her into Kalispell. He could always suggest they have dinner before or afterward, but any of the local restaurants were out. He might like the residents of Fairborn, but there'd be talk. And he'd never enjoyed being a hot topic on the rumor mill.

After racking his brain, he'd come up with a great idea. There was a law-enforcement dinner coming up next weekend, with dinner and music. He could invite her to attend with him, telling her that he needed a plus-one, which might play down the whole date thing.

And today was the perfect day to ask her.

After dropping off the kids at the Tiny Tykes Preschool, he drove down Elmwood Drive on his way home. As he neared the drugstore, he spotted a white pickup double-parked in front. He was off duty today, but both his job and town safety were always his priority. So he pulled into a newly vacated parking space two cars down—and next to his aunt Carlene's blue minivan. She must have left Uncle Ralph at the market to run some errands in town.

Brandon shut off the ignition and got out of his Jeep, just as a young man hurried out of the drugstore with his keys in hand and approached the truck he'd left unattended.

"Sir," Brandon called out, "you're double-parked. I'm not in uniform, but I can still cite you."

"I'm sorry," the man in his twenties said. "I couldn't find a parking space, and I knew I wouldn't be long. I had to pick up an antibiotic and a pain reliever for my baby boy. He's got a fever and an ear infection."

When it came to sick kids, Brandon had been there, done that. He certainly understood the worry, the need to make things better.

"Consider this a warning," he told the harried daddy.

"I will. Thank you, Officer." The man opened the door and climbed inside. He drove off, just as Aunt Carlene walked out of the drugstore, a frantic look on her face, as she scanned the sidewalk in both directions.

"Carlene," Brandon said, "what's the matter?"

"Betty Sue took off again. And I've looked all over for her."

"She's not in the drugstore?"

"No, not anymore. She was standing beside me while my friend Sharon and I were talking about the police dinner you're going to attend, then Betty Sue said she wanted to check something out. But when I went to look for her, she was gone." Carlene snapped her fingers. "Just like that."

"Okay, don't panic." His aunt and uncle were the best of folks. After taking custody of Brandon when he was thirteen, they'd treated him as their own son. And when he'd returned from college with the two babies, they welcomed him home. They also looked after the twins whenever he was on duty.

So it wasn't a surprise that, without hesitation, they'd taken in Betty Sue, Ralph's aunt, an older woman with a tendency to wander. Like his Uncle Ralph always said, "We'll never turn our back on family."

"Don't worry," Brandon said. "I'll look for her. She couldn't have gone far."

He'd no more than opened the driver's door to climb into his vehicle when his cell phone rang. He looked on the console where he'd left it and spotted Betty Sue's name on the display. He answered quickly. "Hey, Auntie. Where are you?"

"I got a little light-headed and figured that my blood-sugar level had dropped."

Brandon sucked in a deep breath, then slowly let it out. "So you left the drugstore?" That wasn't good. Someone would have been able to help her there, but not if she collapsed on the sidewalk. "Where are you?"

"I'm on my way to Darla's. I figure you're still in town after dropping off the kids at preschool. So why don't you join me? There's a nice table by the window. When you get here, I'll treat you to a jelly doughnut."

Had it been a Tuesday or Thursday, Brandon

would have jumped at the chance to see Marissa again. "I'll pass on the doughnut," he said. "I'm not big on sweets. But don't go anywhere. I'm coming to get you."

While wiping down the counter at the doughnut shop, Marissa noticed Betty Sue rushing past the front window as if she was on a mission, which was a little unexpected. It was even more surprising when the bell over the door jingled as she entered, her dyed-red curls held away from her face with a long, sunflower-print scarf.

She'd dressed colorfully again today, choosing a lemon yellow tunic over a pair of green polyester slacks and navy blue sneakers. A beaded, macramé purse hung from her shoulder.

"Good morning, Betty Sue." Marissa glanced out the window, wondering if someone was with her. From what she'd seen, the Tiptons kept a pretty close eye on her, especially Carlene. "It's nice to see you in town."

"Ever since Ralph took the car keys from me and then sold the moped, I don't get out this way very often. But Carlene had an errand to run today, so I rode with her." A rebellious glimmer in her eyes softened the wrinkles on her face. "I didn't know you worked on Mondays."

"Darla's husband had a doctor's appointment

this morning. She's going to relieve me around ten or eleven."

Betty Sue moseyed toward the display case and studied the doughnuts, Danishes, muffins and cinnamon rolls. "Is that cherry filling in those jelly doughnuts?"

"Yes, it is."

"Good. I love cherries. And Doc Clemmons told me I should be eating more fruit."

Marissa stifled a grin. "How can I help you?"

The older woman looked up and smiled. "Hopefully, I can help *you*."

Marissa had no idea what she meant by that, but before she could ask, Betty Sue turned away and craned her neck to peer out the window that faced Elmwood Drive.

Her behavior seemed a little odd today, but then again, from what Marissa had seen and heard, Betty Sue was a bit of a novelty.

"Are you waiting for Carlene to join you?" Marissa asked.

"She could show up, I suppose. And she'll probably be a little snippy-snappy when she does." Betty Sue headed for one of the white café-style tables near the window, pulled out a chair and took a seat. "I was at the drugstore a few minutes ago. While I was looking for my favorite brand of hair color, I ran into Darla. She was waiting on a prescription for her hubby and mentioned you were working today, which surprised me."

"Actually, I help Darla out whenever I can."

"Aren't you a sweetheart." Betty Sue looped the strap of her purse over the back of her chair and let it hang. "I noticed someone put out a water bowl on the sidewalk. I figured it was you."

"A lot of pet owners walk their dogs up and down this street," Marissa said. "And I thought the dogs might appreciate a drink."

"Like I always say, someone who's kind to animals and children must have a pure heart."

Marissa would like to think so, even though there were people in her past who'd questioned her heart. "Can I get you something to drink while you wait, Betty Sue?"

"Sure. I'd like a large hot chocolate with extra whipped cream."

"You got it."

"You told me you were single," Betty Sue said. "That hasn't changed, has it? I mean, you haven't started dating anyone yet?"

Why the curiosity? Had Brandon sent her on a fact-finding mission? And if so, should she be flattered?

On the other hand, maybe Betty Sue was just inquisitive, if not outright nosy.

"No, I'm still not dating anyone." Marissa turned her back and began to fill Betty Sue's order. She had no more than squirted an extra dollop of whipped cream into the hot chocolate when the bell on the front door jingled again. A familiar voice sounded, and her heart took off like a shot, and she froze.

"Aunt Betty," Brandon said, "Carlene's been calling you. She was worried when you left the drugstore without telling her. And even more so when you didn't answer her call."

"Oops. I must have had the ringer on silent, Brandon. Sorry about that. You remember my friend Marissa, don't you?"

Marissa slowly turned around, a disposable cup of hot cocoa in her hand.

At that, Brandon spun around and faced the display case. A slow, endearing smile stretched across his face and dimpled his cheeks.

"Hey," he said. "I didn't expect to see you here."

"Brandon," Betty Sue said, "don't just stand there gawking at the pretty woman. Tell her what you'd like to order."

He blew out a weary sigh. "I wasn't gawking. I was just surprised to see her, that's all." He sat at the table, across from Betty Sue, then turned to Marissa. "I'll have a large coffee. Black."

Marissa nodded, glad to have something to do because he *had* been gawking, at least a little. Hadn't he? She proceeded to pour his drink into a to-go cup. Then she took it to the table, just in time to catch a furrow on Brandon's brow and a mischievous twinkle in Betty Sue's eyes.

As she placed the drinks in front of them, Brandon offered Marissa an apologetic grin, although she wasn't sure what he had to be sorry for—other than being too darned gorgeous for a woman's own good.

She might be wrong, but it seemed as if Betty Sue was trying to set the two of them up, although she wasn't very smooth.

She ought to be annoyed, she supposed, but it was kind of cute. And if truth be told, the fact that someone in Brandon's family seemed to like her was a huge relief.

But did *he* like her?

The bell jingled, the door swung open again and Carlene entered, scanning the room until her gaze landed on her aunt.

"Oh, for goodness sake," Carlene said, her voice laced with both frustration and relief. "You scared the ever lovin' liver out of me again. Please, please, *please* stop taking off on a tangent without telling me where you're going."

Betty Sue rolled her eyes. "I would, but I can't very well do that when I'm not sure where I'm heading."

Marissa, who stood silent while watching the scene unfold, glanced at Brandon. When their eyes met, they shared a mutual moment of silent laughter.

Betty Sue whispered something to Brandon, then gave him a nudge before getting to her feet. She made her way to the front of the store, where her niece stood. "I love you, Carlene. And I'm sorry I worried you. Where's your car?"

"It's parked in front of the drugstore, right where I left it."

"Good. Let's go home. Do you want any coffee or hot cocoa to go? Maybe a bag of doughnut holes we can share during the drive?"

Carlene let out a weary sigh. "Sure, Auntie."

Marissa kept quiet as she filled the order: coffee with cream and sugar and a dozen doughnut holes.

"Did you still want a jelly doughnut?" Marissa asked the older woman.

"You bet I do. Doctor's orders and all." She winked, then reached into her macramé bag, pulled out a black wallet with a peace-sign appliqué on it and withdrew a twenty-dollar bill. "I'm springing for Brandon's coffee, too. And once I get our doughnuts, Carlene and I will leave you two alone."

Marissa would be happy to be left alone with Brandon. And if her luck held out, she wouldn't have another customer for a while.

* * *

Betty Sue sat in the passenger side of the mini-van, munching on the jelly doughnut and preparing herself for a scolding. She'd always been a rebel, which had set off her parents more times than not. And since Carlene seemed to have taken on that same role with her, she couldn't help being troublesome.

"I need you to stop wandering," Carlene said. "You scared me half to death!"

"I'm sorry. I guess you could say that I just get a wild hair every once in a while." Betty Sue stuck her finger in her mouth and sucked off the sugary glaze. Mmm. Darla served a mean doughnut.

"Mama told me that you were the most strong-willed and adventurous woman she'd ever known."

True.

"Ralph and I worry about you," Carlene added. "You're not as young as you used to be, Auntie."

Betty found that it was usually in her best interest to keep quiet at times like this. When she did, her niece and nephew usually just let it go and chalked it up to Betty just being Betty, always marching to her own drummer. Everyone had been shocked when she'd agreed to move in with her niece and her husband. But she'd tried living in one of those so-called active-senior facilities and had been terribly disappointed to find that there'd been very little to no action there.

Just a lot of old people, shuffling around waiting for the next bingo game. But Betty wasn't ready for that.

Besides, it was nice to be around family, especially since she'd never had kids. Of course, neither had Ralph and Carlene. But they'd raised Brandon ever since he was thirteen. And speaking of Brandon…she hoped that he was happy now that he was sitting with that lovely doughnut lady.

Once Betty Sue and Carlene left the doughnut shop, Marissa turned to Brandon. "Betty Sue is a real hoot. I really like her."

"She's hard not to like, but she really frustrates Carlene. To be honest, I think she does it on purpose. Betty Sue has always been an independent woman, and she's not ready to hand over control to anyone, especially Carlene."

"I'm sure it must be hard to give up your independence." Marissa paused, then bit down on her bottom lip. Should she address the subject that had grown clearer and more obvious as the last few minutes had worn on?

She may as well. Brandon had to have noticed it, too. "I don't know about you, but it seems to me that Betty Sue is trying to do a little matchmaking."

"She wasn't very subtle, was she?" He scooted his chair away from the table, then made his way to the front counter. "But I *would* like to ask you out."

Okay, she thought, as she leaned in to him, waiting. Wanting.

"There's a special dinner to honor law-enforcement officers in the county on Saturday night. And I wondered if you'd like to go with me. As my plus-one."

Her gut clenched, and the heat that had begun to simmer in her body cooled. *Law-enforcement officers?* Why would Brandon be attending an event like that? Was he an attorney? Or…

Her cheeks warmed, her mind screamed no and her heart spun in her chest like the tires of a car stuck in the mud. Surely, he wasn't a member of the police force. Was he?

He had to be. Right?

If the words hadn't stalled in her throat, she would have asked him flat out if he was a cop.

"That is," he said, "unless you're seeing someone."

She sucked in a wobbly breath. "No."

"No, you aren't seeing someone? Or no, you're not interested in going to that dinner?"

Both. How did she tell him she'd be a hot mess if she was expected to eat and socialize with a roomful of law-enforcement officers?

And what would he say if she told him why?

She sucked in a breath. Okay. Enough. It was

time to put the past behind her, right? She wasn't a frightened teenager anymore, with nowhere to go, no one to turn to.

But she couldn't. Instead, she said, "I'm sorry, Brandon. It sounds like a nice evening, but I already have plans for Saturday night."

He looked a little surprised, if not deflated. And she felt crappy, as if she'd lied to him. But she hadn't. Neither had she been forthright. Should she say something? Or keep her secret to herself?

Not that it was anyone's business. "Then maybe another time," Brandon said, his cheeks a little rosy as if he'd been a high-school freshman who'd asked the prom queen out on a date, only to be rejected.

She felt his embarrassment, which drew her sympathy and battered her resolve.

"Sure," she said. "Maybe another time."

A slow grin spread across his face. "All right." He nodded, took a step back, then turned and walked out the door.

She watched him go, her heart racing, thumping like the frantic footsteps of someone resisting arrest. At the same time, her heart crumpled.

There went a great guy with the wrong job. Brandon was out of her league on so many levels—his community standing, for one. Financial security for another. And even if that didn't matter to him, there was no way a former felon ought to even consider dating a cop.

Chapter Four

Marissa hadn't seen Brandon in nearly a week, but she'd soon learned why he'd invited her to a law-enforcement dinner. He was a deputy sheriff, one of several who patrolled the Fairborn city streets.

If he'd had another job—anything other than one that sometimes locked up innocent people—she would've been happy, maybe even excited, to go out with him. To dinner or anywhere. But there was no way she'd consider dating anyone remotely connected to the criminal-justice system, no matter how hot he was. And Deputy Brandon Dodd, with those broad shoulders, lively green eyes and square-cut chin, was a definite hottie. But Marissa's experience with the police, lawyers and correctional guards tipped the scales out of his favor. Way out of his favor.

She hadn't heard from him since, so she figured he'd gotten the message and realized she was reluctant to date him. But the following Tuesday morning, while she was working at Darla's, he showed up in uniform.

Just the sight of him sauntering in the door sent a rush of adrenaline through her veins, kicking up a fight-or-flight response.

Calm down, girl. You haven't done anything wrong.

"Good morning," Brandon said with a charming grin that was a little disarming.

She managed a smile and said hello in a voice that came out a little too squeaky for comfort.

Her attempt to act normal and unaffected must have failed, because his happy expression shifted to a furrowed brow, and he zeroed in on her like a cop cornering a suspect.

"What's the matter?" he asked.

Unwarranted guilt swept over her as if he'd just caught her robbing the till, but she shook it off the best she could. She *wasn't* guilty of anything. Not now, and certainly not before.

"Nothing's wrong. What can I get for you?

Coffee? You take it black, right? Maybe a jelly doughnut?"

"Yes. And just coffee, please. But that's not why I'm here."

Uh-oh. Was he here on official business?

"What's up?" she asked.

"I wondered if you could answer a couple of questions."

Her heart pounded. Did she need a lawyer? She hadn't done anything wrong, but she'd learned the hard way that innocence didn't matter if no one believed her. "Officially?"

"Sort of."

Her heart hammered harder and louder, as if trying to escape. Had he somehow found out about her past? It was doubtful, she supposed. But she didn't dare ask.

"You're here alone, right?"

"Yes. Is that against some town ordinance? Am I in some kind of trouble?" she asked. *Darn it. What was the matter with her?* She hadn't meant to look or sound guilty.

He stammered. "I didn't mean to imply that I was here in an official capacity."

Was this some kind of *Bachelor Cop* reality show? "I'm sorry. Your uniform kind of threw me off."

He tugged at his collar and cleared his throat. "Damn. This is going badly. I'm sorry. I haven't done this sort of thing in years. And it's definitely not like riding a bike."

His nervous response downsized her apprehension. He was right. This was going badly.

"I'd like to go out with you," he said. "And I thought we were both on the same page. But when I asked you to attend that dinner with me last Monday, I got the feeling that you weren't interested in going out with me. And I just wanted to clear the air."

She couldn't blame him for that. If she intended to be a permanent resident and businesswoman in Fairborn, she'd need to tamp down her nervousness around him and anyone else who worked in law enforcement.

"I have a lot on my plate right now," she said. "Two jobs, an online college course, helping Alana get ready for the farmers market, then manning the booth with her on the weekends. There's also the wedding I'm planning, which is really important to me. So I'll need to help Alana choose a florist, a baker. And since Callie, her best friend, is about to give birth to twins, I might have to go shopping with her to pick out a dress."

She heard herself rambling, but what other tasks could she throw at the guy so she could dodge a more truthful answer? Ordering tables and chairs from a party-rental place in Kalispell? No, that'd be too much.

"I'm sure you're busy," he said. "But please be honest. Are the kids a problem for you?"

At that, her lips parted, and her bluster fizzled. "No, of course not. You have great kids. Cute, sweet."

"Then, it's me?"

No. It wasn't that…

"It's *me*," she said. "You're a great guy, Brandon. Handsome. Bright. Easy to talk to. And your kids are…" Oh, for Pete's sake. Now she was talking herself into it!

She threw up her hands, as if in surrender, and conjured another, more believable excuse. "I'm coming off a breakup, so I'm not up for getting involved with anyone so soon." Not that she and Steven had been all that invested, romantically speaking, and the decision to split had been mutual. On top of that truth, mocking her lame excuse, last summer wasn't all that recent.

The longer he stood there, studying her with a sympathetic eye, the more she began to regret telling him she'd had plans last Saturday night. Not that she would have gone to that police dinner with him. She would have felt as out of place as a pole dancer at a ballet recital.

The door jingled, and two middle-aged women entered. When they spotted Brandon, they both broke into broad smiles. The tallest one, a brunette, said, "Good morning, Sheriff. I can see you're here for your doughnut fix."

Brandon gave them each a polite nod. "Hello, Sharon. Danielle. I'm actually a deputy. The sheriff is an elected position. And that would be my boss."

"I know," the brunette said, "but Danielle was just telling me that she heard Sheriff Beaumont is thinking about retirement and that you'd like to take his place."

"That's just a passing thought."

"Well, you'd have our vote," the blonde—Danielle—said.

The women approached the display case, where Marissa stood rooted in place.

"Good morning," Marissa said, shaking off the idea of deputies and sheriffs and elections—oh, my. "What will it be today?"

The brunette, Sharon, glanced at Brandon. "I'm sorry. We didn't mean to take cuts, Deputy Sheriff."

The other chuckled. "That's right. We know how important a doughnut break is to you guys."

"Go right ahead," he told them. "I've already had my break. I was just leaving. Have a good day, ladies."

He tossed Marissa a parting grin, one that didn't seem to reach his eyes. Then he walked out the door.

Sharon nudged her friend, then winked at Marissa. "All in a day's work, huh?"

But it wasn't. Not really. And when Deputy Dodd sauntered into Darla's, whether with his kids or on duty, it was never a typical day.

Brandon climbed behind the wheel of the squad car, shut the driver's door and blew out a sigh of frustration. He hated stereotypes, yet he'd just validated the one about cops and doughnuts. The only reason he'd gone to Darla's today, for a fix he didn't need, was because it was Tuesday.

And he knew Marissa would be there.

Only trouble was, after focusing his life on his kids, he was a little rusty at dating. Still he'd given it his best shot this morning. Apparently, the question had stunned Marissa, and he wasn't sure why. He'd assumed she'd felt that same little zing he'd felt, the same attraction.

But he did understand how a recent breakup might cause her to drag her feet, fearing she might make the same mistake again. Hell, he was still reluctant to get involved with anyone, and his split with Julie had been three years ago.

Marissa also might have shied away from him because of his job. If that was the case, it would have been nice if she would've just leveled with him.

It was also possible that she wasn't ready to go with him to something so formal. Then again, maybe he'd read way too much into her pretty smile and her kindness to his kids. Maybe she just wasn't that interested in him, after all.

He'd always prided himself on being observant and a good judge of character. Or course, that instinct had let him down when it came to dating Julie.

But his gut told him Marissa wasn't like that. She couldn't be. Jimmy and Maddie had taken to her right away. She put out bowls of water on the sidewalk for the dogs whose owners walked them past Darla's.

Either way, he thought as he backed out of the parking spot and headed down Elmwood Drive, he'd tripped up somehow.

And to make matters worse, he was in such a hurry to hightail it out of the shop, he'd left without taking his cup of coffee.

The trusty, old maroon Honda Civic had well over a hundred thousand miles on it when Marissa bought it six years ago, and up until now, it had been dependable, getting her from San Diego to Montana, so she couldn't complain. But she had a feeling there were some big repair bills coming her way.

The battery had been dead this morning, and she'd needed a jump start. And even after she'd gotten on the road and started the twenty-minute drive to town, she hadn't been able to go any faster than forty miles an hour.

The air-conditioning hadn't ever worked, not since she bought the car, and so she'd rolled down the windows. But the weatherman had predicted a warmer than usual summer day, so she'd dressed appropriately—a white scoop-neck blouse with lace trim, black shorts and a pair of sandals. She'd also put her hair in a ponytail. But she'd begun to perspire. Even the soft rock playing on the radio failed to keep her mind off her growing discomfort.

As she turned off the county road and onto Fairborn Drive, the engine rattled and chugged.

Now what?

She turned off the radio so she could pay more attention to the noise under the hood. She'd need to explain it to the mechanic at Don's Auto Works.

Would she even make it there? She had her doubts.

At the intersection, she stopped and waited for the red light to turn green. Once it did, she pressed down on the gas pedal, but instead of taking off, the car inched forward, chugging and sputtering as it did.

"Darn it," she uttered as she urged it across the intersection and to the side of the road, where it conked out completely.

At least she only had a couple of miles to walk.

She grabbed her purse, as well as her water bottle, and got out of the car. No need to lock it, since there was nothing of value inside—and it wasn't going anywhere. Then she started her trek into town. She'd barely gotten a hundred yards when she spotted a squad car up ahead.

Apparently, the officer—Brandon Dodd, she assumed—spotted her, too, because he turned around and drove her way.

Sure enough. It was Officer Hottie. He rolled down the window. "Car trouble?"

"Yes. I'm afraid so. I was going to walk to Don's Auto Works. Hopefully, they'll have a tow truck available." She tucked a loose strand of hair behind her ear. "Is it okay that I left my car on the side of the road? I mean, I don't want to get a ticket. I can try to push it to a better spot."

"It's okay where it is. But there's no need for you to walk. Get in. I'll give you a ride."

She hesitated as she eyed the vehicle, with its red light on the top and caged back seat. She hadn't ridden in one of those in years, and she didn't plan to ever again.

"It's okay. I don't mind walking. I can use the exercise."

"Don't be silly. It's going to be warm today."

It wasn't just warm, it was supposed to be a scorcher. And she'd be a sweaty mess by the time she got to the repair shop.

"Climb in," he said.

"Front or back?"

He laughed as if he didn't know she'd been half-serious. "The front, of course."

Reluctantly, she opened the passenger door and got into the squad car. In spite of all the gadgets on the dash, which were a bit disconcerting, the cool air blowing through the vent welcomed her, urging her to relax and accept the ride he'd offered her and the comfort it provided.

As Brandon pulled back onto the road and headed toward town, he said, "I hope my aunt's attempt at matchmaking didn't bother you too much."

"It didn't. In fact, I get a kick out of her. She's one of a kind."

"You can say that again!" He chuckled. "Betty Sue is actually my great-aunt. On Ralph's side."

Marissa wasn't sure how those relationships worked.

"Family is family," she said, although hers had never really counted her as such.

"My aunt and uncle watch the twins for me when I'm on duty," he added. "And now they're looking after Betty Sue."

"They seem like wonderful people."

"They're more like a mom and dad to me," he said.

She was tempted to ask what happened to his

parents, but she wasn't up to sharing her own past with him. So she kept quiet.

"I put Maddie and Jimmy into preschool three days a week, in part to give my aunt and uncle a break, even though they insist they don't need one."

Hoping to dig for a little more information, she asked, "Does their mother help out with them?"

"She's not involved in their lives. I have full custody."

Wow. She hadn't seen that coming.

"So what about you?" he asked. "Do you have family?"

"We've never been very close."

"That's too bad," he said.

She didn't see it that way. Having no family— or an estranged one—was better than claiming the lousy one she'd once had. She'd rather not explain why her family had turned their backs on her— and why she'd cut them out of her life after that. But maybe she'd better explain, at least a little.

"My mother died when I was a baby," she offered. "And my father died in a freak industrial accident when I was twelve."

Brandon inhaled, looking surprised. "I'm sorry. That must have been a tough loss. Did you have any extended family members who took you in?"

"No. Not really." She would have been better off if there had been aunts, uncles, grandparents…

"My dad remarried a couple years before he died, so my stepmother raised me." No need to go into any more detail than that.

"I'm lucky," he said. "My parents split up, and the divorce sent them both into tailspins. If I had stayed with either of them, there's no telling how I might have turned out. But I was lucky. I moved in with Ralph and Carlene, and they showed me what a real family was like."

"That's cool." It was too bad Marissa hadn't had her own extended family who'd taken custody of her when her father had died.

Maybe, instead of spending time behind bars and being uneasy around judges, attorneys and the like, she might have ended up patrolling the city streets like Brandon did.

As they neared the auto-repair shop, Brandon shot a glance across the seat. "Do you have a ride home?"

"Actually, I'm working an extra shift at the salon today. It's only a couple of blocks away from the auto repair shop, so I'll walk."

"And after that? What if your car isn't ready?"

She'd figure something out. Maybe ask someone to give her a ride.

Before she could respond, he said, "I'll tell you what. I'll stop by the salon later this afternoon and make sure you have transportation."

"You don't need to do that."

"I know. But I'm off duty at five thirty. And then I'm going to drive out to the market to get the kids. So it's right on the way."

Dang. Did Officer Hottie have to be such a regular guy? And so darn thoughtful?

"Sure. Thanks. That'd be nice. I have a feeling my car will be in the shop for a long time."

As she slid out of the passenger seat, he said, "One more thing. Would you be opposed to going out to lunch with me? Not today, of course."

Seriously? That sounded tempting, but she was too stunned to speak.

"If that seems too much like a date," he added, "how about a picnic with the kids at the park?"

To be completely honest, the thought of packing a picnic basket and taking Jimmy and Maddie to the park was really appealing. She'd like to watch them run and play, push them on the swings, stand at the foot of the slide and cheer them on the ride down…

"That sounds fun," she said. Besides, an outing like that would also be a lot safer because it would take the focus off them as a couple.

And it wouldn't feel like a date.

By the time six o'clock rolled around, the salon had closed, and the stylists had all left. Tameka was in the back room, talking to her husband on the phone.

Marissa was just restocking the inventory that was displayed next to the front desk when Brandon knocked at the locked front door. She'd expected him to drive up in his squad car and show up in his uniform, but he was dressed in a pair of worn jeans and a black T-shirt. It was a surprisingly normal ensemble that, along with a dimpled grin, set off a swish and a flutter in her chest.

She placed the last of the conditioner on the glass shelf, then she opened the door and let the gorgeous deputy inside the shop.

"What did you find out about your car?" he asked.

She blew out a sigh. "I'll be on foot or borrowed wheels for a while. At least a week."

"That's too bad," he said. "Are you ready to go?"

"Yes. I just need to let Tameka know I'm leaving. She's in the back room, tallying up the receipts for the day." Marissa left Brandon at the front of the store, then slipped into the back room, where Tameka had just zipped the cash bag shut. "The shelves are all restocked. Do you need me to do anything else?"

"No, I've got things under control. Thanks again for coming in on your day off, Marissa. And you've been a lifesaver on Wednesdays and

Fridays. I might even need you to work on Saturday afternoons—if you're available."

She helped Alana at the farmers market on the weekends, but Alana would understand if she had to leave early. "Just let me know when you'd like me to start. Have a good evening."

"You, too."

Marissa headed back to the front of the shop. And to her ride home.

Moments later, she was opening the passenger door of Brandon's personal vehicle—a white late-model Jeep Grand Cherokee that had two boosters secured in the back seat.

But what surprised her was a cardboard pet carrier resting between them. A whimper sounded from within.

"What's this?"

"A puppy. I just picked him up a couple of minutes ago. The kids have been begging for a pet, and I found him wandering around this morning. His fur was so dirty and matted that it looked like he'd been on the street for a long time. So I took him to the groomer, a friend of mine from high school. She's a real dog lover. After she fed him and gave him a bath, she had the vet who volunteers at a rescue center check him out. He's healthy, but a little underweight. And since he doesn't have a microchip, we have no way of finding his owner. So I plan to surprise the kids."

"Lucky dog," she said. And she meant that. The puppy was going to live with a great family.

Marissa had always wanted a pet, although her stepmother had refused to even consider it. But she would have settled for a nice family. As it turned out, she hadn't gotten one of those, either.

"Do you mind if I take him out of the box? I don't imagine he likes being caged." Marissa certainly hadn't liked it.

"Sure. Go ahead."

After loosening the lid, she reached in and pulled out a small black-and-white cocker spaniel mix. "Oh, my gosh! He's so cute."

The pup squirmed in her arms, but only so he could reach up and give her a long, appreciative lick on the cheek.

"What are you going to do with him when you work and the kids are at preschool?" she asked.

"Mrs. Hendrix, my neighbor, is a dog lover. I called her and asked if she'd be interested in being a puppy-sitter, and she was more than a little enthusiastic. So I've got that covered."

She wasn't surprised that he had it all figured out. To be honest, she wouldn't mind puppy-sitting, either. That is, if he ever was in a jam. But she didn't dare offer. She'd have to be careful about getting too close to him and his family.

"Are you in a hurry to get home?" he asked.

The question took her aback. "Why? What do you have in mind?"

"I can't wait to surprise Maddie and Jimmy. So I thought I'd stop at the market first, give them the puppy, and then the kids and I can drop you off at the ranch before the three of us head home."

"Where is home?" she asked.

"The kids and I live in town, over on Second Avenue. When the sheriff's office hired me, I bought a house with a big backyard. I even built them a playhouse. They love it there, and so do I. But they don't get to spend as much time there as I'd like them to."

"Because of childcare?"

"Yes. I mean, they love Uncle Ralph and Aunt Carlene. And they've got a playroom in the back of the market. But it's…"

"Not home," Marissa supplied.

"No, it's not. But there are a lot of other single parents doing the best they can to create a home. The twins are happy and healthy, so we're doing okay."

Marissa had to admit, she'd begun to like the man behind the badge, even if she was still a little uneasy around him. There was just something about the way he looked at her that made her wonder if maybe…if there was a chance that her past wouldn't freak him out.

"So what do you say?" he asked. "Would you

rather have me drop you off first? Or do you want to see the kids go crazy over their new pet?"

Part of her, the part that wanted a man like Brandon to like her and to include her in a family activity, wanted to say yes. But the other part—the part that would never forget the time she'd spent in jail—insisted that she hold her tongue.

What would he think if he knew of her arrest? Would he, like her so-called family and most of the people she used to know, believe that a conviction in and of itself automatically meant guilt?

But when she looked into his warm gaze, her fear and questions seemed to dissipate into the pheromones dancing in the cab of the Jeep, along with the scent of his mountain-fresh cologne.

A deputy sheriff was bad enough. But he was running for county sheriff. An elected position, with the respect of everyone in the community. She ought to decline, but in spite of her better judgment, she wanted to share in the children's delight, so she said, "Sure. Let's take this sweet bundle of fluff to meet his new family."

Chapter Five

Brandon gripped the steering wheel and studied the road ahead as he drove to the market to pick up the twins. He was glad Marissa had agreed to ride along with him. She seemed eager to introduce the puppy to the kids, but she'd been giving him mixed signals when it came to going out with him.

He glanced across the console at her striking profile, as her big brown eyes gazed out the windshield. She wore red lipstick today, instead of the simple pink gloss she favored when working at Darla's. And her hair, which she often pulled up in a twist of some kind, hung soft and loose, the glossy curls tumbling over her shoulders. She looked classy but casual.

Beautiful.

He sucked in a breath. She'd probably be a knockout no matter how she dressed. Even stepping out of the shower, her face clean, hair dripping wet, her skin...

Whoa. Now, there was an image he'd like to see. And one he was going to have a hell of a time getting out of his head. Not that he planned to work too hard at it.

Up ahead, a Greyhound bus pulled off the side of the road in front of them. It stopped near the awning-covered bus stop. Several passengers got on, while a woman, a blonde with long, stringy hair, got off carrying a small, black canvas tote. She had on a bulky, oversize gray sweatshirt and a pair of baggy jeans.

Marissa craned her neck, as if checking out the new arrival.

"See someone you know?" he asked.

She turned and cast him a wistful smile. "No. Not really. Just someone traveling alone. And no one was waiting for her."

He'd noticed that, too. In his line of work, being observant was critical.

"Why did she catch your attention?" He assumed Marissa might have once traveled alone, once been nervous or scared to embark on a journey to a new life in an unfamiliar community.

She shrugged. "No reason. It's just that she seemed…kind of sad, I guess. That's all." She lifted the puppy and snuggled it. "I guess it's because I have a heart for strays."

"Like Alana," he said. The woman she lived with, the one who'd inherited the Lazy M, renamed it Rancho Esperanza and had let various people move in with her, all of them having a need of one kind or another.

"Alana has a big heart, and she's been a good friend. It's hard not to smile when she's around, and more so now. She's in love and excited to be getting married."

Alana was a little too trusting, if you asked him. But he wasn't one to warm up to people too quickly. As a cop, he'd learned to be skeptical at first. Of course, his experience with Julie had led him to be cautious, too.

"Speaking of marriage," he said, "how are the wedding plans coming along?"

At that, Marissa's somber expression brightened. "So far, so good. Alana liked my idea of placing a gazebo near a weeping willow tree on the property, and Clay has already purchased the lumber and materials to build it. He can afford to hire someone, but he wants to do it himself and plans to start work on it this weekend."

Brandon—like a lot of men he knew—didn't see the point in having big weddings. It seemed to him that the enormous amount of money spent on a party could be put to better use. But most women seemed to make a big deal out of them—planning them, dressing up to attend one.

His mood darkened. Not Julie, though. When she told him she was pregnant with the twins, he'd offered to marry her, but she'd turned him down, saying she didn't see any reason for it, that it wasn't necessary. And, as things panned out, that decision had ended up for the best. A divorce would've made their split much harder. And more complicated.

He wondered where she was. Still in New York, he imagined. She never called, never asked about the kids. That was for the best, too, he supposed. But it ate at him to think she'd just walked away from them, abandoning them completely.

Minutes later, he and Marissa arrived at Tip Top Market, which was about to close. Brandon assumed his aunt and uncle were getting ready to lock up and go into the back room to count the day's receipts. That would leave Betty Sue and the kids alone in the house. He always tried to pick up the kids and be home before his great-aunt was left alone with them, but stopping by the salon and waiting for Marissa had taken a little more time than he'd expected.

Not that he was overly worried about the twins. Carlene was the one who'd mentioned her concern about Betty Sue, especially as she was growing older. But the kids adored Auntie, and she loved them, too.

He swung along the back side of the store and drove down the short, blacktop-paved lane that led to the modest, three-bedroom house where his aunt and uncle lived.

"So this is where you grew up?" she asked.

"I spent my teen years here."

"Where were you before?" She kissed the top of the puppy's head, then quickly added, "I'm sorry. That's none of my business."

He wasn't sure why he felt compelled to open up, to share his past with her, but she was easy to talk to, and he couldn't see any reason to keep it from her. "Up until I was thirteen, I lived with my mom and dad. He was verbally abusive, and they both had drinking problems. They probably still do. I decided I wanted more out of life than a crappy past and an unpleasant future. So I called Uncle Ralph and asked if I could move in with him and Carlene. They'd never had kids of their own and didn't blink an eye at taking me in."

"I'm impressed that you made such a wise decision when you were still a kid."

He shrugged, unwilling to mention that his

mother, like Julie, had let him go without much of a thought.

"I'm sure you've made Ralph and Carlene proud," Marissa added, her voice soft, almost wistful.

"I tried." He didn't usually talk about it to people who didn't already know, but... "During my junior year in college, Uncle Ralph was in a car accident and almost died. I quit school and came home to help Carlene with the market."

"You didn't graduate?" she asked.

"I did, eventually. Uncle Ralph was out of commission for nearly a year and had to go through extensive rehab. Once he was able to spend a full day at the market, he and Carlene insisted that I go back and get my degree. I'd wanted to complete my education, too, so I appreciated their full support."

He'd no more than parked in front of the house, when Maddie ran outside, the screen door slamming behind her. "Daddy!" she squealed in glee. "You're home! Come see what we made."

Brandon glanced at Marissa and winked. "Welcome to my world. And just to warn you, whatever they made probably resulted in a huge mess. According to Maddie and Jimmy, they love being left with Betty Sue because she's the only grown-up who has time to play with them."

"That's sweet." Marissa reached for the cardboard carrier. "Do you want me to put the puppy in the box so you can surprise them?"

"No. I doubt that little guy wants to go back in."

"You're right." Marissa opened the passenger door and got out of the Jeep.

"Jimmy!" Maddie hollered into the house. "Come quick. Daddy brought the doughnut lady here!"

At that, her brother ran out onto the front porch, with Betty Sue on his heels. The moment they spotted the black fur ball in Marissa's arms, their eyes widened.

"You got a puppy!" Maddie said.

"Can we play with it?" Jimmy asked.

Marissa shot a glance at Brandon, allowing him to share the news with his kids, then she set the little pup on the ground.

"I found this little guy on the side of the road," Brandon said. "He doesn't have a home, so I thought we might want to keep him."

Both kids gasped, then raced to where the puppy sniffed, checking out his surroundings. Jimmy was the first to reach the little stray and knelt beside it. Maddie, as usual, was a bit more reserved. "We get to keep it? For reals?"

Brandon nodded his agreement. "Yes, for *reals*. But having a pet is a big responsibility. So I asked Mrs. Hendrix if she'd watch him for us when you're in school and I'm at work."

"I love dogs," Betty Sue said. "I had three of them when I lived in Missoula. I also volunteered at the Humane Society. The puppy will be in good hands with me."

Brandon didn't doubt that for a minute. "Thanks, Auntie. We can bring the pup here once in a while. But Mrs. Hendrix lost her dog last spring, so she's looking forward to having a puppy to look after and to keep her company."

Betty Sue began to kneel beside the kids, then straightened and grimaced as if her arthritis objected to childish enthusiasm. "So what are we going to name him?" she asked the children.

Maddie, who was in a real princess phase, plopped down in the dirt, between her brother and the little stray. "If he was a *she*, we could give her a name like Ariel or Jasmine or Belle or…"

"Oh, no." Jimmy picked up the dog and gave it a hug. "He's not a princess. He needs a boy name. Like Thor."

"He does *not*." Maddie placed her hands on her hips. "He needs a *dog* name, like…" She bit down on her bottom lip, then looked at Betty Sue. "Help us."

Clearly delighted to be asked, Betty Sue beamed. "Your favorite book is *Where the Wild Things Are*. So how about Max?"

"I *love* that name," Maddie said. "And I love our new dog."

"Me, too." Jimmy giggled when Max licked his face. "Hey. He loves me back."

"Let's go, kids. I need to drop Marissa off at Rancho Esperanza, then we'll take Max home and help him get settled."

Moments later, the kids were secured in their booster seats, the dog resting beside them.

"I wanna hold Max," Jimmy said.

Maddie objected. "You got to pick him up first, so I get to hold him in the car."

Before Brandon could settle the dispute, Marissa said, "Why don't you take turns? Maybe you can trade off every five minutes."

Brandon tossed her a smile. "Great idea. You're a good referee."

"I suspect anyone who's around these two very long would have to be." She laughed, then climbed into the passenger seat.

He was glad she'd been a part of his surprise for the twins. In fact, there was a lot to like about her, but she'd made it clear that he'd have to take things slowly.

Five minutes later, as Brandon turned into the drive that led to the ranch, Marissa said, "Time's up."

The twins giggled and passed Max between them.

Brandon's time with Marissa was nearly up, too, he thought as he pulled into the yard at

Rancho Esperanza and put the Jeep in Park. He glanced in the rearview mirror, where the kids seemed oblivious to anything other than Max.

He hadn't planned to walk Marissa to the door, but… On the other hand, why not? It would give them another chance to talk one on one, without little ears listening. So with the engine running and the air conditioner on low, he left the kids and the puppy in the car. "I'll just be a minute," he told them.

Then he and Marissa got out of the Jeep and walked up the steps and onto the front porch, where he could still keep an eye on the twins.

"Thanks for bringing me home." She offered him a shy smile that damn near turned him inside out.

"No problem. And thanks for holding Max. And being the timekeeper for the kids."

At that, her smile broadened, lighting up those golden-brown eyes and sparking something inside him, something warm and blood-stirring. He reached up and cupped her jaw. His thumb brushed her cheek, and her lips parted as if she sensed he was about to kiss her. He waited a beat, but she gave him no indication that she was going to object.

He might regret it later, but he brushed his lips across hers. He hadn't meant to do more than give her a sweet good-night kiss, but when her lips parted, he was toast. It must have affected her in the same way, because the kiss exploded into an array of fireworks that could put the Fourth of July to shame.

She placed her hand on his chest, then slowly drew her mouth from his. "That's not taking things slow."

No, it wasn't. He might have pulled her back into his arms and kissed her again, but he had two curious children in the back seat who might see them.

"You're right." But he wasn't about to apologize. And he didn't think she expected to him to. "I'll talk to you later. When the kids aren't with me. Neither of them can keep a secret."

Then he gave her a parting grin and returned to the Jeep.

And speaking of secrets…

When it came to his feelings for Marissa, he knew he'd better keep them close to the vest until he found out whether she felt the same way about him.

The next day, Marissa went to work at Darla's. Each time the door opened, she looked up, expecting to see Brandon walk into the shop. He'd told her they'd talk later, and she'd been dreading that little chat, especially if he brought up the kiss they'd shared.

The truth of the matter was, she'd enjoyed it. Way too much. And her hormones had nearly run amok.

It was amazing how one sweet but alluring kiss could be so tempting. Nevertheless, she wasn't about to get romantically involved with a police officer, no matter how sexy he was or what a good kisser he was.

After spending the morning serving doughnuts and coffee at Darla's, Marissa walked to the deli down the street. She planned to meet Alana at the Petal Pusher so they could pick out flowers for the wedding. She had an hour to kill, so she decided to buy a sandwich and eat it at the park across the street.

She'd no more than walked into the eatery when she noticed a blonde with long, scraggly hair checking out the menu that was posted on the wall. The twenty-something woman wore a gray, oversize sweatshirt—the same one she had on when she'd gotten off the bus last night.

It had to be the woman she'd seen when she was with Brandon. But what she hadn't been close enough to notice yesterday was a red, swollen gash on the side of her head and a thick coating of makeup that didn't do a very good job of hiding a black eye.

As she began to count out her change, Marissa said, "Hi, there. You must be new in town."

The woman nearly jumped out of her skin. Then she glanced over her shoulder apprehensively. When her tentative eyes met Marissa's, she offered a frail smile. "Yes. Sort of. But I'm... really just passing through."

Marissa nodded, as if that made perfect sense. She'd felt the same way when she'd arrived in Bakersfield, California. And then again in both Reno and Boise as she made her way to the perfect place to start a new life.

She suspected the blonde wasn't just passing through. Running away was more likely. And probably from the person who'd caused her injuries.

Marissa didn't like to make assumptions about people she didn't know, but she couldn't tamp down the sympathy for the skittish drifter that sprang up from the depths of her own battered soul.

The woman reached into the front pocket of her jeans and pulled out a couple of wrinkled bills and a handful of change. As she began counting it out, Marissa said, "Put your money away. Your lunch is my treat."

Her lips parted, and her brow furrowed. "You don't need to do that."

"Yes, I do. On my first day in town, a nice man purchased my lunch and told me it was his way of welcoming me to Fairborn. So I want to pay his kindness forward. And maybe someday, if you get the chance, you can do the same for somebody else."

"I…" Her apprehensive, disbelieving expression morphed into one of relief. "Thanks. I don't know what to say."

"You don't have to say anything. My name is Marissa. What's yours?"

"Ella."

After purchasing turkey sandwiches, potato chips and apple juice for both of them, Marissa suggested they eat at the park. When Ella agreed, they crossed the street and found an unoccupied picnic table under the shade of an elm.

"You don't owe me any explanations," Marissa said. "But I have a feeling you're running away. And if someone hurt you, I don't blame you at all."

Ella keep her gaze down as she continued to unwrap her sandwich.

"I ran away from someone, too," Marissa added. "And it took me five years and three different towns before I found the perfect place to call home."

Ella cut a glance her way. "Someone hurt you?"

"Pain and abuse isn't always physical." Marissa unscrewed the lid of her apple juice and took a swig.

Ella remained quiet for the longest time, then she said, "It was my husband. I vowed to love him in sickness and health—and all that stuff. So I took his anger and beatings for as long as I could. Besides, he told me if I ever left, he'd kill me. And I didn't doubt him. But two nights ago, he came home drunk and…" She took a deep breath and slowly let it out. "I swore that would be the last time he hit me. So when he fell asleep on the sofa, I took the keys to his pickup, grabbed what little I could carry and climbed out the bedroom window. After throwing his keys down the well, I made it to the bus depot and spent half the money to buy a one-way ticket as far as I could get."

"And now you're in Fairborn."

Ella nodded. "But it's not far enough. I'm scared to death that he's going to find me…"

Marissa didn't doubt her fear for a second. When she'd spent time in jail, she'd met a woman who'd been charged with murder after killing her abuser because she'd felt as though it was her only escape. "Do you have a plan? Someplace to go?"

Ella slowly shook her head. "Not really. He'd look for me at my mother's house first. And he knows my friends."

"Have you called the police?"

Ella shook her head. "He's a cop, and those guys tend to stick together. I know most of them are good people and have a high sense of morals and ethics. But anytime I see a man in uniform, I cringe."

Marissa's gut clenched. She knew exactly how Ella felt. Not the physical abuse. But the uneasiness around police officers. "I don't want to get into it now, but I know what you're saying, and I can relate." They exchanged a smile, and that gave them a bond of some kind.

"Maybe I can help you. Give me a minute." Marissa got to her feet, and as she walked a short distance away, she reached into her purse and pulled out her cell phone. Then she called Alana.

When her friend answered, Marissa told her about Ella and her need to find a place to hide.

Just as she'd expected, Alana said, "I'm heading to town. But we're not going to meet at the Petal Pusher. Wedding flowers can wait. Meet me at The Mane Event. A complete makeover is in order."

"Agreed." Marissa ended the call and returned to the table. She placed a gentle hand on Ella's shoulder. "I've got your back, honey."

Tears welled in Ella's eyes. "Why are you helping me? And being so nice? You don't even know me."

"Because women stick together. And it's the right thing to do."

Fifteen minutes later, Ella and Marissa—once strangers but quickly becoming comrades-in-arms—entered the salon, where Tameka was manning the front desk.

"Does someone have time for a color and a cut?" Marissa asked. "My friend wants a brand-new look. And it's my treat."

As soon as Alana arrived at the salon, Marissa introduced her to Ella, who was waiting for Robin to finish combing out her client before taking Ella back to her station.

"I've talked it over with my fiancé," Alana said. "You're welcome to stay with us. But you'll need to clean up after yourself. And there'll be no drug use, no boyfriends…"

"You don't have to worry about that," Ella said. "I've never used drugs and don't intend to start now. And I doubt if I'll ever trust another man again."

"Then, it's a deal," Alana said. "Welcome to Rancho Esperanza."

Then they left Ella in Robin's capable hands and walked to the florist, where they studied an array of blooms and photos. They even found time to stop at Patty Cakes, the bakery on Elmwood Drive, where they set up a tasting.

An hour and a half later, they returned to the salon, where Ella's long blond hair had been dyed black and cut in a short pixie style. Bangs hid the injury on her forehead. The only thing that re-mained the least bit familiar was a pair of cautious blue eyes, a smudge of makeup hiding the bruise under one of them.

"Ella," Marissa said, "you look amazing." Then she turned to Robin. "You're a whiz. I'm so glad you had time for her."

"Me, too," the stylist said. "We've had a busy afternoon, and we're really going to be slammed until we close."

Marissa handed Robin a twenty-dollar tip. "I'll settle up with Tameka."

Ella smiled shyly. "This is the first time I've felt remotely safe, Marissa. Thank you so much. I promise to pay you back."

"Don't worry about it. It was my pleasure." Various people along the way had supported Marissa, in one way or another, on her journey from felon to future businesswoman. She reached into her purse, pulled out her wallet, removed her ATM and handed it to Tameka. "Here you go."

As Tameka ran the card, she asked, "Would you mind watching the phones for me, Marissa? I just cracked a crown, and it's super sensitive. The dentist is going to fit me in. If you can't do it, that's okay. I'll see if my sister can cover for me while I'm gone."

"I'd be happy to help out, but…" Marissa shot a glance at Alana, who was going to take her home since the car was still in the shop.

"No problem," Alana said. "I don't mind waiting. There's something else I'd like to do while we're in town."

"Oh, I almost forgot," Tameka said before stepping away from the counter. "I'm going to need you to work on Thursday afternoon along with your regular shift on Friday. Are you available?"

"Yes."

"That's great. I don't want to stretch you—or my budget—too much. So why don't you take tomorrow off?"

"All right." That would give her and Alana time to address and mail out the invitations, along with taking care of several other items on her wedding to-do list.

While Tameka headed toward the back of the shop, where she always parked, Marissa stepped behind the counter. "Thanks, Alana."

"No problem. Ella and I are going to take a walk down to Wear It Again, Sam."

Ella appeared confused. *"Where?"*

"It's a consignment clothing store," Alana explained. "They carry some neat stuff, and you're going to need a few outfits."

"But I don't…" Ella sucked in a shaky breath. "I mean…"

"Don't worry, honey." Alana took Ella by the arm. "It's what we do at Rancho Esperanza. We help each other out." As they started for the door, Alana glanced over her shoulder. "We'll be back in an hour or so. If you get out sooner than that, meet us there." Then she led Ella out of the salon.

After they left, The Mane Event continued its buzz of activity, with clients coming and going. A sign out front announced that walk-ins were welcome, but the three hairstylists, as well as the manicurist, were booked back-to-back for the rest of the afternoon, so if anyone showed up, hoping to get in today, they were out of luck.

Of her two part-time jobs, Marissa enjoyed this one the most. It was cool to see people coming in haggard or scruffy, only to walk out looking their best.

The time flew as Marissa juggled appointments, purchases and departing clients. She'd barely gotten a moment to breathe when she saw Carlene Tipton entering the salon with Betty Sue. Carlene looked rather plain in a pair of jeans and a plaid blouse. But the older woman practically lit the room. A coral-and-green-striped scarf held her wild red curls away from her sparkling eyes. She wore a multicolored bohemian skirt and a white top with a large flamingo appliqué on the front. A pair of bejeweled slippers rounded out the eye-catching ensemble.

Marissa greeted them with a smile. "Good afternoon, ladies."

"I'm here for a manicure and a pedicure," Carlene said. "And my aunt has an appointment with Hailey for color."

"Jordan, the manicurist, took a short break between clients, but she should be here any minute." Marissa turned and surveyed the back of the busy shop, where Hailey stood at her station, blow-drying a woman's hair. "I'm afraid you'll both have to wait. But it won't be long."

"I see an empty chair back there," Betty Sue said. "I'll just sit myself down and watch the activity until Hailey's ready for me."

"Auntie," Carlene said, "I think it'd be better if you sat up front with me."

Betty waved her off. "You and I are all talked out after our drive to town. I'd like to chat with someone else for a change."

Carlene let out a sigh. "Okay. That's fine. But don't leave the salon."

Betty Sue let out a humph. "Would it be okay if I went to the bathroom?"

"Auntie, you went before we left home."

"I don't have to go *now*. Not yet, anyway." Betty Sue looked around and said in a loud whisper, "But I took a laxative this morning."

Carlene cleared her throat. "Of course you can go to the bathroom. But will you give me a heads-up first?"

Betty Sue laughed. "Sure. No problem. Thank you for your interest in my plumbing." The older woman winked, then made her way to the back of the salon, where she took a seat next to the shampoo bowls.

Carlene leaned forward, resting her arm on the reception desk, and spoke quietly. "I hope you don't think I'm mean or short-tempered. I'm usually very patient. But Betty Sue exasperates me at times. I know she means well, but…"

"I understand," Marissa said, although she did think that Carlene seemed pretty irritable when she was with her aunt. She probably ought to loosen up a bit.

Carlene blew out a sigh. "Betty Sue begged me to get her a hair appointment, but when I did, she made me change it several times for silly reasons. I mean, why should it matter when my nephew is on duty? It's not like my husband can't handle babysitting the kids and running the store. Ralph's got things under control—and most of the time, better than I do."

"Maybe you need a break," Marissa said. "Or some help. You've got a lot on your plate—running the store, chasing after two sweet but active preschoolers, not to mention Betty Sue."

"You're probably right. I even thought it might help to hire someone to work at the market, although it's such a big part of our lives that I hate to take a step back."

"Well, you're here now," Marissa said. "So

relax and enjoy. Maybe, while you're waiting, you can look at the display of polish on the wall and pick a color."

As Carlene walked away, compassion washed over Marissa, and she wished there was a way for her to help. It had to be difficult to run a store, babysit a couple of adorable but precocious pre-schoolers and keep up with Betty Sue. Yet a bit of envy struck her, too. It would be nice to belong to a family—one that cared for each other and had each other's backs. There was a time she would have given anything to belong to a family like Brandon's, even if they were all a little unusual.

Carlene returned to the desk, holding a bottle of red polish, and lowered her voice. "And do you know what else? I don't even need to get my nails done today, but I didn't dare leave my aunt here on her own. With my luck, I'd come back to find she'd hitchhiked to New York to attend a Wood-stock reunion. Or go try to find another moped. And to make matters worse, she would never pull one of those stunts on Ralph!"

Betty Sue was quite the rebel. Marissa smiled and said, "I'll keep an eye on your aunt so you can kick back and enjoy your beauty treatment."

As if on cue, Hailey's last client approached the desk to pay for her treatment, which meant Betty Sue was next.

Several minutes later, Jordan returned from her

break and took Carlene to her station for the manicure and pedicure. So Marissa got back to work, collecting payments from customers, answering calls and making appointments.

Periodically, she glanced at Hailey's station, where Betty Sue's color was applied. So far, so good. Marissa looked at Carlene, who was getting her pedicure while waiting for her fingernail polish to dry, and gave her a thumbs-up. Then she got back to work, organizing the products on the shelf next to the cash drawer.

That is, until one client let out a shriek. "Hey! My casino winnings are gone!" Still draped in a black robe to protect her clothing, her hair wrapped in a towel, the fifty-something woman marched up to the reception desk, her finger pointed at Marissa. "Someone got into my purse while I was at the shampoo bowl!"

Marissa's heart pounded in a primal beat—a flight-or-fight response. She threw up her empty hands, almost in surrender. "I didn't take anything. I haven't even left this desk."

"I know that. I wasn't accusing you, honey." The client waved her off, then jabbed her index finger at the telephone. "You need to do something."

"I'll do it," Betty Sue hollered from the back of the salon. "My nephew will get to the bottom of this."

Marissa had absolutely no reason to feel guilty. Or nervous. But tell that to her raging heart rate.

But all this didn't make sense. Who would've stolen money from that woman's purse?

And why did Brandon have to be on duty today?

Chapter Six

Dispatch sent Brandon to The Mane Event to check out a reported theft. Since Marissa didn't work on Tuesdays, he hadn't expected to see her there. But when he walked inside and spotted her standing behind the front counter, looking especially pretty with her hair pulled up in a messy topknot and her lipstick worn down to faint pink tinge, time stalled until he realized that he was damn near gaping at her, and he snapped back to reality.

"What's going on?" he asked.

"One of our clients said someone stole money from her purse." Marissa pointed to where a frowning woman in her fifties sat in a chair near the front window, her cheeks flushed, her graying hair wet and stringy.

Betty Sue, whose red curls had been styled neatly, was sitting in a seat next to the alleged victim, clutching her macramé purse in her lap. A few steps away, Carlene lounged at the pedicure station, her bare feet outstretched, rolled tissue between her toes, the nails lacquered in bright red polish.

Were his aunts involved?

The woman, who still wore a protective black cape over her shoulders, got to her feet and placed her hands on her hips. "I'm glad you're here, Deputy. Someone stole my casino winnings—nearly five hundred dollars!—while I was at the shampoo bowl. I was going to show Robin pictures of my new grandbaby, and when I dug through my wallet, I noticed my money was gone. I'd counted it earlier today, so I know it was in there. And now it's not."

"No one has left the salon yet," Marissa said.

Unless the thief had slipped in and out the back entrance, then he or she was still on-site.

"If someone got into my purse," Betty Sue said, "I'd look to see if I'd misplaced my money before making a big stink."

That certainly was possible. His great-aunt was

a little absentminded at times and often misplaced her things.

The victim tossed his aunt a dirty look. "Mind your own business, Betty Sue."

Clearly, the two women knew each other.

"Aw, come on, Rosanna." Betty Sue clicked her tongue. "Last week, when we played bingo, you couldn't find your wallet in that big ol' suitcase you call a purse. And then come to find out it was there all along."

"That's an expensive designer bag, I'll have you know."

"It's a knockoff."

"That's enough, ladies." Brandon glanced at Rosanna's feet, where an oversize jungle-print tote rested. Then he met her gaze. "Is that your purse, ma'am?"

The woman nodded. "Yes, it is."

"Do you mind if I look inside?" he asked.

Somewhat miffed, she reached for the leather handle and handed over the bag. "Knock yourself out."

Damn. It weighed a ton. Betty Sue was right. He opened it to look inside and dug through a slew of things like chewing gum, loose coins and safety pins, a small pack of tissues, breath mints and a roll of antacids. He even found two sets of car keys, not to mention a crossword-puzzle book and a small box of chocolate-covered raisins. He finally found her wallet at the bottom, and like she said, there wasn't any cash in there.

He then unzipped a side pocket, reached into it and pulled out several folded hundred-dollar bills and some twenties. "Is this the money you were talking about?"

She flushed a dark shade of scarlet. "Um… Yeah. That's it."

Betty Sue rolled her eyes. "Another mystery solved."

Brandon hated to add insult to injury, but he couldn't help it. "Ma'am, you really ought to take the time to search your belongings before accusing someone of stealing. It could lead to hurt feelings and other unintended consequences."

The woman nodded, grabbed her purse from Brandon, then walked out of the salon, her hair wet and stringy, her shoulders still draped in the black cape.

"Look at that," Betty Sue said. "Now who's the thief? She didn't pay for her haircut. And she's wearing the salon's cape. Want me to chase her down?"

"That's not necessary." Brandon figured she'd return the cape and pay for her cut as soon as her embarrassment died down.

"Betty Sue," Carlene said, "why in the world would you call 9-1-1 when a simple search of that woman's purse would've put the issue to rest?

Brandon has more important things to do than to chase after imaginary thieves."

Betty Sue had been the one to call dispatch? His aunt was truly something else.

Betty Sue's smile slipped into one of wide-eyed surprise. "Uh-oh. Nature's calling." Then she hurried to the back and disappeared into the bathroom.

Carlene blew out an exasperated sigh. "I'm sorry about that, Brandon. But you know how she is."

"No problem. Not every call I get ends up with an arrest." He turned to Marissa, who appeared to be a little unsettled by the incident. "I'm just glad Rosanna found her money."

"Me, too," Marissa said. "It's nice to know there isn't a thief in our midst."

"For the most part, you'll find the people who live in Fairborn are law-abiding and trustworthy."

She fingered her necklace, a small silver heart on a delicate chain.

"Are you okay?" he asked.

She blinked and dropped her hand. "Yes, of course." Her smile and sweet demeanor returned. "Thanks for responding so quickly."

"All in a day's work." Which reminded him. He was still on duty and had a job to do. So he tore his gaze from hers. He turned toward the door.

Then he had a second thought. "I've been meaning to ask. What'd you find out about your car?"

She rolled her eyes and blew out a sigh. "Besides needing a new battery and a starter, replacing the spark plugs and a few other things? Let's just say that Prudence will be in the shop for a while."

"*Prudence?* You named your car?"

She gave a little shrug. "Why not?"

"No reason, I guess." Actually, it was kind of cute. His gaze swept over her. In fact, everything about her was cute.

"I told the mechanic to go ahead and fix it," she said. "My only other option is to buy another vehicle that has fewer miles on it. So I'll be catching a ride to town for a few days."

He'd seen her car, and poor Prudence had seen a lot of miles and better days. "How'd you get here today?"

"Clay, Alana's fiancé, brought me. And Alana is going to drive me home. She's just down the street. Shopping."

"Good. I'm glad you've got it covered. When do you have to work in town again?"

"Not until Thursday. If my car isn't ready by then, I'll ask either Clay or Alana to bring me to work."

"No need. I'm going to drop off the kids at the market early that morning. You can ride with me."

Her lips parted, and she slowly shook her head. "You don't need to do that."

"But I'd like to. Besides, it's not out of the way."

She thought about it for a moment, then she seemed to see the rationale. "Are you sure you don't mind?"

"Not at all." There was nothing Brandon wanted to do more than to spend some time alone with her. To let her know he wasn't like the guy she'd once been involved with, the guy who'd broken her heart and betrayed her trust.

And he hoped to set a date when the two of them could go out, no matter if it was at dinner or lunch.

A real date—and without the twins.

While Carlene drove the family minivan back to the ranch, Betty Sue lowered the passenger-seat visor, lifted the curls off her forehead and peered at her reflection, checking out the residual dye on her forehead. It was her fault, though. When Rosanna had freaked out, Betty Sue hadn't been able to stay seated, so she'd jumped up before the stylist had time to clean it. She'd wanted to be where the action was.

Hmm. Next time she was at the salon, she'd have to tell the stylist not to take too much off the top. Her curls got a little wild sometimes, so they needed to be tamed. But she didn't want them whacked off.

"Betty Sue," Carlene said, drawing her attention from her reflection, "how do you know that woman who thought her money was stolen?"

"Rosanna? She plays bingo on Wednesday nights." The woman had also made a brazen play for Earl Hoffman, the bartender who worked all the events held at the Grange Hall. And Betty Sue had already made her interest in him known. So she and Rosanna had some heated words about it a time or two.

"I got the feeling that you suspected Rosanna might've forgotten where she'd stashed her cash."

That's because it had happened to her a few times before. "Rosanna's a little ditzy, which is why she can't keep a boyfriend."

"Boyfriend? What are you talking about?"

"Oh, nothing. But let's just say her card is a B-12 short of a Bingo."

Carlene clicked her tongue. "If you knew she was that ditzy, why did you call 9-1-1 as if there'd been an armed holdup in the salon?"

Betty Sue chuckled. "I wouldn't have made a fuss if Brandon wasn't working today."

"Oh, for goodness sake. You did it on purpose? Are you trying to set him up with Marissa?"

"She's a nice girl."

"You hardly know her."

"I get vibes about people." Betty Sue closed the mirror and raised the visor. "And I have a *real* good one about her. She's not ditzy like Rosanna."

"You can be a little ditzy yourself," Carlene said.

Hmm. Maybe. But at least Betty Sue could still pull the wool over Carlene's eyes. Because her bossy niece believed that Wednesday nights at the Grange was called Bargain Bingo, when it was actually High Roller Bingo, with a cash bar. And both Betty Sue and Rosanna had hit it big last Wednesday.

"Don't you ever get feelings about people?" Betty Sue asked, although she knew the answer. Her niece was about as observant of her surroundings as someone playing six different cards during Blackout Bingo.

Carlene blew out a sigh. "I wish I did. But I don't. About six or eight weeks ago, we had a customer come into the market. He bought a pack of cigarettes and a couple of lollipops. I assumed he had kids and pegged him for a decent sort. But it turned out that he and a buddy assaulted Clay Hastings, stole his car and left the poor man for dead. And I never saw *that* coming."

"From what I heard, neither did Clay." Betty Sue chuckled at her dark-humored quip.

Carlene chuffed. "Oh, Betty Sue. Really! But I won't argue with you about Marissa. She seems to be a nice woman. And the twins like her, which is a plus. But please don't interfere in Brandon's love life."

"I was just trying to help."

"You don't need to. And if you promise to back off, I'll let you in on a little secret."

Betty Sue loved secrets. "What's that?"

"I talked to Ralph last night. And he assured me that Brandon likes Marissa and plans to ask her out. But if you don't stop interfering, you're likely to put a stop to things before they're off and running."

Betty Sue lifted her hand in a Boy Scout salute. "It's a deal. But will you and Ralph please keep me in the loop? I love hearing about budding romances." Especially when her vibes told her that a man and woman were perfect for each other.

And, in that case, there was no harm in helping the relationship along.

As soon as Tameka returned to The Mane Event, she thanked Marissa for covering for her while she was away. "The receptionist at my dental office said she'd squeeze me in, but I had no idea it would take so long."

"No need to apologize. I'm glad I was able to help." Marissa reached for her purse. "It's never fun to sit in a dental chair, but it's better than having a toothache."

"Don't I know it?" Tameka placed her own purse where Marissa's had been, on the top shelf, under the front counter. "I assume everything went smoothly while I was gone."

"Sort of." As she and the salon owner traded places, Marissa shared the details of Rosanna's mistaken claim and Betty Sue's knee-jerk reaction that had led to the deputy's arrival.

"Oh, boy." Tameka rolled her eyes. "I'm glad I missed the excitement. Thank you so much for handling it."

"All in a day's work," Marissa said, inadvertently repeating the response Brandon had made earlier.

"Thanks again," Tameka said.

"You're welcome. I'll see you on Thursday." Marissa pushed open the salon door and stepped onto the sidewalk.

Alana and Ella hadn't returned yet, so she began the walk to the consignment store, planning to join them unless she met them along the way. She'd only gotten two blocks down the street when she spotted Alana and Ella up ahead, chatting away like two old friends. Ella carried a bulging white bag, filled with her purchases.

The three met on the sidewalk in front of the two-story redbrick building that housed Fairborn Savings and Trust, the bank that occupied the entire first floor.

Ella reached up to tuck a strand of hair behind her ear, a habit she'd undoubtedly acquired before cutting it short. Her hand dropped back to her side, and she looked first at Alana, then at Marissa. "I don't know how to thank you guys for all you've done for me."

"We've both had people help us along the way," Alana said. "So we like to do the same for others whenever we can. Come on. Let's go home."

At that, they walked to Alana's car, a brand-new one Clay had recently purchased for her to replace the old ranch pickup she used to drive.

As they approached the white SUV, Ella said, "You have no idea how long it's been since I've had someone in my corner."

Marissa could certainly relate to that.

"Maybe now you can stop looking over your shoulder," Alana said.

"I wish I could. It's just that the last time I ran away, Doug found me two blocks from the bus depot. He grabbed me from behind and dragged me to his truck. And when we got home, he beat the crap out of me and swore he'd kill me if I ever tried a stunt like that again. And I had no reason to doubt him. I just couldn't take it anymore."

"You'll be safe at Rancho Esperanza," Alana said.

True. But it would probably take a while for Ella's fear to die down. She might have undergone a makeover that left her looking much different on the outside, but on the inside, where she bore the emotional scars of her abuse, it would take time to heal and move on.

Marissa ought to know. She still carried a few emotional scars, even if no one had physically abused her.

She'd no more than reached the passenger door when a barrage of memories struck, one after the other. She squeezed her eyes shut, hoping that might block out the painful images.

A drug-sniffing dog.

Police officers swarming the car.

Her hands pulled behind her back, handcuffs snapping shut, the metal cold and tight against her skin.

It's not mine, Marissa had cried. *I don't know where it came from.*

But no one had believed her, least of all her so-called family. Nor had they cared enough to come to court during the trial, let alone pay for a decent lawyer. The public defender had taken very little interest in fighting for justice in her case.

Needless to say, once she'd served her time and completed her probation requirements, she'd left San Diego and her past behind. But it had taken nearly five years and several moves for her to finally find a place where she could put down roots. And she'd never looked back.

Well, not until Erik's text a couple of weeks ago.
Damn you, Erik, she thought. *And damn your father and my stepmother, too. I never want to hear from any of you again.*

That night, as Marissa was crossing the living room on her way to the kitchen to help Alana prepare dinner, her cell phone dinged, alerting her to an incoming text. She reached into her back pocket and pulled out the smartphone. When she glanced at the lighted display and spotted the 619 San Diego area code, she froze in her tracks.

Call me. It's important.

Oh, no. Not again.
She'd yet to open the text completely, but she'd seen enough to know that Erik hadn't given up on his attempt to contact her. She'd meant to block his number, but she'd gotten so busy that she'd forgotten. Before she could read the rest of his message or get into her settings to block him now, the doorbell sounded.
"I'll get it," she called out.
She was still stunned by Erik's text when she swung open the door, only to find Brandon standing on the stoop and sporting a dimpled smile.
She glanced around the porch. "Where are the kids?"

"I left them and Max with Mrs. Hendrix, my neighbor." He took a step back. "Can I talk to you? Alone?"

"I...uh... Sure." She tried her best to return his grin with one that was unaffected, but she doubted that she'd been able to completely pull it off. Nevertheless, she walked out onto the porch, the screen door closing behind her. The sun had just begun to drop into the west, streaking the Montana sky in swatches of pink and lavender.

"What's up?" she asked.

"I wanted to talk to you, but I didn't want to do it while you were at work or in front of an audience." He glanced at the living-room window, just as Ella was walking through the room, probably on her way to help Alana in the kitchen.

"Who's that?" he asked.

"Her name is Ella. She's staying here for a while."

"Oh, yeah? Is she a friend?"

Did it matter? "Just someone we're helping out right now."

Brandon scrunched his brow. "You don't have any qualms about inviting a stranger to live with you?"

"Yes, but not Ella."

"Why not?" His eyes bore down on her.

"Because. We just don't."

"Based on what?"

Marissa wasn't usually so trusting. Heck, she'd had a good reason not to be. But Alana had been so good to her that her pay-it-forward philosophy was hard to ignore. And Ella definitely needed a friend right now. "Just call it gut instinct. She needed a place to live, and we want to help."

"Con artists are experts at making you feel comfortable before they pounce. I can run a check on her through the database."

Is that what he'd done with her? Did he already know about her record?

No. He would have said something, right? And he certainly wouldn't have asked her out.

"Thanks," she said. "I appreciate your concern, but there's no need to run her through your database. Ella's fine. And so are we."

"I'm just trying to look out for you."

And she appreciated that. It wasn't often that anyone had cared about her enough to do that.

She studied the handsome deputy, who'd shed his uniform for a pair of worn jeans and a white, crisply pressed button-down shirt, the sleeves rolled up.

"Are you always so trusting?" he asked.

"Are you always so skeptical?"

"I have to be."

She supposed he did. She'd crossed paths with a lot of skeptics when she'd gone through the criminal-justice system. And while she understood they were just doing their jobs, their suspicious natures made her a little skittish.

"I didn't mean to question your judgment," Brandon said.

He had a point, though. "No offense taken."

"I came here to ask you a question."

"What's that?"

"I'd like to take you to dinner. There's a nice steak house in Kalispell. It's got great reviews, and I'd like to try it out, but I don't want to go alone."

"Are the kids going, too?" she asked.

His smile fell. "It's not a kid-friendly place."

"I thought we were going to take things slow. And that our first... I mean, what happened to the picnic at the park we'd talked about?"

"Don't you think that, before we involve the kids, we should take time to get to know each other a little better?"

She supposed that made sense. He probably didn't want to risk confusing the children if their...date—or whatever it was—didn't work out.

"We can always take the kids on a picnic some other time," he added.

She hadn't gone out to a nice dinner in ages. Not since her father died. She wasn't even sure she had anything appropriate to wear. She could probably find something, though.

Yet her reluctance to date a police officer

wouldn't let her speak, even though he looked like a regular guy right now, one who was more handsome than a man had a right to be.

Would going out with him be so bad? What was she really afraid of? He might be a deputy sheriff, but it's not like he'd been her arresting officer.

His expression sobered. "Why don't you sleep on it? I'll see you later."

Then he turned and headed for his Jeep, looking a little dejected. She had half a notion to call him back, but she remained on the porch, watching him go.

As he pulled out of the yard, a heavy blanket of guilt draped over her.

If Erik hadn't just sent her that text, dredging up old memories and throwing her off balance, she might have agreed—whether Maddie and Jimmy went with them or not.

Truth be told, she liked Brandon. And she liked his kids, too. Their family didn't include a mommy, but that didn't mean they hadn't made the best of it. They were happy.

She and her father hadn't needed a mother, either. They'd been happy, too, until Suzanne entered the picture. Fake tan, fake blond, fake boobs, all of which could be forgiven. But not the fake smiles she had for Marissa whenever Daddy was around.

Thank God those miserable days were over.

Maybe that's what drew her to Brandon—in addition to sexual attraction. His family. And he was offering her a chance to get to know them, too—if not to become a part of it. And then, there was that kiss... That amazing, heart-strumming kiss.

She slapped her forehead. What a dingbat. She was going to jinx things if she wasn't careful. Sure, she might have a past, but if she wanted to put it behind her, she'd have to embrace the future. And that meant taking a risk.

So how did she make things right with him?

She supposed she could start by telling him about her conviction and the time she'd spent in jail—before he decided to run her name through his database. And if he still wanted to date her, then she'd go to dinner with him on Saturday night.

Feeling better already, she returned to the house with a spring in her step and tomorrow's game plan in mind.

Chapter Seven

When Brandon left Rancho Esperanza after talking to Marissa, he wanted to go anywhere but home. Thirty minutes earlier, he'd left the twins and their puppy with Leanne Hendrix, the rosy-cheeked widow who lived three doors down from him. Leanne had moved in six months ago, and she'd already proved to be a good neighbor—one of the best.

"I'm going to see a friend," he'd told her before leaving his house. "So I might not get home until late. There's leftover spaghetti in the refrigerator."

"I brought some homemade chocolate-chip cookies for dessert. So don't worry about us. And don't rush on my account. If you're not home before eight, I'll get them ready for bed. Then I'll watch TV until you get back." She scanned the living room. "Where are the little munchkins?"

"They're in the backyard, playing with Max. I've already told them I'm leaving."

"So get going." She lifted her hands and shooed him toward the door. "I'm glad that you're finally getting out. You need to do that more often. I just hope that friend is a lady."

His smile had given his secret away, but that hadn't concerned him. Leanne Hendrix was more discreet than most of the people who took a personal interest in his love life. And another plus, she didn't socialize with either Carlene or Betty Sue.

They'd be all over him, wondering what had happened, how his new romance was unfolding. But whatever he'd thought was happening between them had hit the wall.

Sure, the kiss they'd shared had convinced him that they had chemistry, but it hadn't swayed Marissa at all. He'd left the ranch feeling confused, frustrated and embarrassed. But rather than go home early and let Leanne know that he'd crashed and burned, he'd stopped by Sully's Pub to kill some time.

He'd no more than stepped in the door when his good friend and local firefighter spotted him.

"Hey, Dodd!" Greg Duran called out, as he motioned for him to join him at his table. "I thought you'd given up the party life for good."

When they were teenagers, neither of them had been what you'd call party animals. They'd both played football for Fairborn High and had tried to stick to a healthy regimen as student athletes. Brandon had graduated as the valedictorian, while Greg had come in a close second. Then they'd both gone on to the University of Wyoming, where they'd kicked up their boots a bit. But in their junior year, Uncle Ralph had suffered his serious injury, and Brandon had filed an incomplete and gone home to help at the market.

Now, as Brandon pulled out a chair at Greg's table, he asked, "What are you doing? Are you all by yourself?"

"I met Joel Braddock here, but he got a call from his wife, and she wasn't very happy that he'd forgotten their anniversary was tonight. I figured I'd finish my beer, then go home." Greg motioned for the waitress to return to the table. "How're the kids doing?"

"They're doing great." Brandon wasn't at all surprised that Greg would ask. Not just because they were friends, but Greg and his sister Nancy were the twins' godparents. "I left them at home with a sitter. I figured I'd…slip away for a while."

The waitress, a tall blonde in her mid-thirties

stopped by and offered Brandon a welcoming grin. "What can I get you?"

"I'll have a Corona and lime."

He and Greg made small talk for a while, about the weather and the latest playoff game, until the cocktail waitress delivered his beer.

"I put an offer in on a house on Cherrywood, and it was accepted." Greg rested his elbow on the table, then leaned back in his seat. "I'm tired of paying off my landlord's mortgage and decided it was time to buy a place of my own."

"Congratulations," Brandon said, although he couldn't quite shake his somber mood.

"I've been dating Shelley Whitaker," Greg said. "Her sister Melanie is going through a divorce. She used to have a crush on you in school. Want me to set something up?"

"No."

"Wow. The twins' mother must have really done a number on you. I can't believe Brandon Dodd is still unattached. And for some reason, he's happy about it."

"I used to be."

"Something changed? What's up?" Greg lifted his glass mug and took a swig of beer.

"Nothing." Brandon fingered the condensation on his bottle.

"You can't fool me, dude." Greg lifted his nearly empty glass and pointed it at him. "You look like you're stewing about something. What is it?"

Brandon sucked in a deep breath, then slowly let it out. "There's a woman who's caught my eye. I know she's feeling something for me. But she doesn't want to date me."

"Hmm. Why's that? You're not too ugly. And you seem like a decent sort." Greg chuckled at his dumb attempt at humor.

"We've got chemistry, that's for sure. When I kissed her the other night, it was off the charts."

"What'd she do? Slap you?"

"No. She enjoyed it every bit as much as I did. At least, I thought she did."

Greg finally seemed to get it, to see the seriousness and realize how much it bothered Brandon.

"I told her to sleep on the idea of going out with me, but that was more or less a parting shot. I really don't expect her to change her mind."

"So what's her problem?" Greg asked. "Do you think it's the kids?"

"At first, I thought it was. I mean, some women might find a single dad with two four-year-olds complicated and someone to steer clear of. But Marissa is great with Maddie and Jimmy. You can sense when someone doesn't like kids. And that woman clearly enjoys being around them. She likes dogs, too. She really took to Max, our new puppy."

"You're right," Greg said. "That doesn't compute."

"I know." And Brandon didn't like the way the numbers were adding up.

"Could it be your job? I mean, a lot of women can't hack the fact that bad guys might shoot at police officers. We both know that the crimes in Fairborn are pretty tame, but not always. You know that. And some women might worry."

It was sure beginning to look like Marissa might be the kind of woman who'd stress about something like that. "You know, when I first asked her out, it was to a law-enforcement dinner. She said no. And when I showed up at her workplace in uniform, she froze up. She claims it's because she's getting over a broken heart, but I don't know about that. I guess I'm not buying it."

"Maybe it *is* you, dude." Greg chuckled, then slowly shook his head in disbelief.

"That's possible, I guess. But I really don't think that's it. Sometimes, I feel like I've known her forever. Then at other times? It's almost as if she's afraid to date me. I'm in law enforcement. I can read people. And it doesn't make sense."

They each took a drink of beer. Then Greg said, "What you're saying is that something about her doesn't feel right."

Brandon hated to admit it, but yeah. He'd nailed it. "Maybe so."

"Have you thought about doing a background check on her?" Greg asked.

"No. I can't do that. I mean, who runs the woman he's interested in through the database?"

"I get that," Greg said, "but I can talk to a friend of mine who's a private investigator. He'd do it as a favor to me."

"I'm definitely curious." After all, she was new in town and didn't seem to have family here. "But I don't know if that's a good idea."

"It's not a bad one," Greg said. "You have two adorable kids, and you need to be careful about who you let into their lives. Plus, you're thinking about running for sheriff, right?"

"I haven't decided to throw my hat in the ring yet." But he'd certainly considered it.

"You'll need campaign donors, and you sure don't want any skeletons coming out of the closet, even if they belong to the woman you're dating."

"The woman I'm *thinking* about dating. I haven't even taken her out once yet. She's dragging her feet, remember?"

"Dude, you're a catch. Why wouldn't she say yes?"

Brandon hadn't planned to check into Marissa's past. Why should he? She was so sweet, so nice, that he didn't think he had anything to worry about. But Greg was right. He did have the twins to consider. And he'd trusted the wrong woman once.

Oh, what the hell. "Go ahead. Talk to your PI friend." Then in spite of his initial reluctance, he added, "Her name is Marissa Garcia, and she's from San Diego. She works at Darla's a couple days a week and also at the salon. She must have a driver's license, and she's taking a class or two at Fairborn Junior College, so they'd have her social security number."

"Got it. I'll let you know what I find out." Greg typed the info into his phone.

Brandon glanced at the clock on the wall, next to a stag's head. "I gotta get out of here." He reached into his wallet, pulled out a ten and laid it on the table. "I'll talk to you later."

Then he headed home. And if Leanne, bless her ever lovin' heart, asked him how his visit had gone, he'd respond with a thumbs-up.

Who said a hand couldn't lie?

With the wedding a mere ten days away, Marissa had planned to get the rest of the details taken care of on Wednesday. But Darla had called last night at six o'clock, saying her husband's doctor had ordered a bone scan at nine the next morning, along with a couple of follow-up tests.

"I'm feeling fine," Fred hollered in the background. "I don't know what all the fuss is about. Or why it has to be done tomorrow. My leg feels fine."

"He does seem to be okay," Darla admitted. "So he's probably right. But I worry about him. And I think the doctor just wants to rule out any problems in the bone."

"I swear," Fred said loud enough for Marissa to hear, "my wife would pack me in bubble wrap if I'd let her."

"It's only because I love you," Darla told him. Then she cleared her throat. "Anyway, is there any chance you can relieve me by seven o'clock, Marissa? I'll have plenty of doughnuts made by then to last all day."

"No problem. I'll be there."

Now here Marissa was, working at Darla's on a busy Wednesday morning. She'd hardly had a chance to breathe, but she did manage to answer a couple of confirmation emails. One was from the party-rental place for the tables and chairs she'd ordered, and another from the florist saying she could definitely provide the flowers and greenery for decorating the white gazebo Clay built. Everything was scheduled to be delivered to Rancho Esperanza the day before the wedding.

At a quarter to nine, Carl Matheson, the elderly veteran and her favorite customer, opened the door. He'd no more than taken a step inside when he spotted her behind the counter. A slow grin stretched across his craggy face. "Well, I'll be damned. You're a nice surprise. And on a Wednesday, no less."

She returned his smile. "Good morning. How's it going, Colonel?"

"I can't complain." The elderly gent continued into the shop, his blue eyes bright, his cane tapping against the tile floor. "I finally got rid of the walker, but I still have to use this." He lifted the cane in the air and waved it like a sword. "At least I can ward off any muggers who don't know who or what they're messing with."

She laughed. "Looks like you're getting back to your fighting weight. I'm glad that hip replacement didn't slow you down too much."

"Yeah, well, my doctor was a little surprised, too. He called me a tough old soldier. And that's true. At least, I'm healing. I might not be too steady on my feet yet, but I'm moving better."

"I'll get your usual, Colonel. Unless you'd like to mix it up."

"You know what? I'm feeling brave today. Give me a large coffee and one of those cream-cheese-filled pastries. And this time, I'll eat it here. I need to rest my bones before I try to walk home." He took a seat at the nearest table while she poured his coffee, adding his usual sugar and cream, and set his Danish on a plate.

As Marissa served him, she was about to ask if he wanted some company when the door jingled, and Ralph Tipton, Brandon's uncle, entered the shop. She didn't know the man very well, but she'd met him a couple of times.

"Good morning," Marissa said, a little more chipper than usual.

"Hi, there."

"Hey, Ralph," the colonel called out. "Are you driving that fancy new red pickup?"

Ralph grinned. "Yep. I bought it last week. What do you think?"

"Nice wheels."

"Thanks."

Marissa craned her neck and caught a glimpse of a shiny red truck.

"It's the first new vehicle I've purchased in a long time," Ralph added as he walked over to the display case and studied it carefully.

"What can I get you?" Marissa asked.

"I'll take one of those bear claws and a large cup of coffee with a splash of cream."

"Would you like it here or to go?" she asked.

"I'd better take it with me." He let out a weary sigh. "I just did the preschool run, but I need to get back to the market. We've got a delivery coming in, and... Well, things can get pretty hectic at times. Carlene and I are going to hire someone to come in and help out a few days a week. In fact, both Carlene and Betty Sue mentioned that you'd be a good fit and that you might be available."

"I wish I could. Between my work here, at the salon and at the ranch, I just don't have any more hours in the day." And that was too bad. Marissa would have jumped at the chance, but her time was stretched to the limit, especially with the upcoming wedding. Then a thought crossed her mind. "My friend Ella might be available. She lives with us at Rancho Esperanza."

"It wouldn't be a full-time position," Ralph said. "At least, not yet. But I'd like to talk to her—and the sooner the better."

"I'll mention it to her as soon as I get home. And if she's interested, I'll bring her by the market later today so you can meet her."

"That would be great. Thanks."

Maybe, if Marissa was lucky, she'd run into Brandon while she was at Tip Top Market. She'd apologize for her hesitation last night. And if he asked her out to dinner again? She swallowed, pondering the conversation she'd need to have with him about her time in jail. But if he was still game, so was she.

At the end of Brandon's shift, as he drove to the market to pick up the kids, the conversation he'd had with Greg just a few hours ago was weighing heavily on his mind.

"I hate to have to tell you this," Greg had said,

"but Marissa Garcia has a record. And she did jail time in San Diego."

"For what?"

"Drug charge. Transporting. A year in county jail. After her probation was up, she moved away from San Diego. She's lived in Bakersfield, as well as Reno and Boise, and eventually landed in Fairborn. And it looks like her family turned their backs on her."

Brandon felt like throwing up. He couldn't believe it. No wonder she seemed hesitant around a member of law enforcement.

She wasn't who he thought she was.

And why so many moves? Whatever her reason, the fact that she didn't stay in one place was another red flag.

He supposed he should be happy to get the real scoop, but it was a hard blow. He'd misjudged another woman, it seemed.

But what had happened? The crime took place several years ago. People could change, couldn't they? And apparently, Marissa hadn't been in trouble since.

Either way, dating a woman who'd been convicted of a crime was out of the question. He had two sweet kids to think about. And a possible campaign to run in the near future.

But that didn't make him feel any better about it. He'd liked Marissa. A lot.

When he pulled onto the parking lot, he noticed a familiar old pickup in front of the market. It had once belonged to Jack McGee, the late owner of the Lazy M, which was now known as Rancho Esperanza. He assumed that Alana Perez was picking up a few necessities. As he turned onto the easement that led to the house, he spotted Uncle Ralph's new pickup parked behind the store and smiled. The man had worked his butt off for years, and for the most part, he didn't treat himself to luxuries. So that Dodge Ram was well deserved. And now it was his pride and joy. *Good for you, Ralph*, he thought. *And heaven help anyone who dares to ding it.*

Brandon continued the short drive to his aunt and uncle's house, where Betty Sue sat on the front porch in one of two rocking chairs, watching the twins playing on the steps that led to the yard. They chattered between themselves while holding small chalkboards in their laps and yellow pieces of chalk in their hands. Max, his weary head resting on his paws, snoozed between them.

Marissa, who'd been seated in the rocker next to Betty Sue, got to her feet at his approach, and his gut clenched. He was going to have to talk to her, and if he could get her off to the side, he supposed now was as good a time as any. Betty Sue often said, "Everyone is redeemable, given enough love and understanding." But the cop in

Brandon, coupled with his experiences, made him question how often that actually happened.

Jimmy brightened and set his chalkboard aside. "Daddy! You're home! Auntie has a bag of lemon drops, and she shared 'em with us. You want one?"

"No, thanks. Not now."

"And guess who came to see us," Maddie added. "Marissa!"

"I see that," he said, unable to match his daughter's enthusiasm.

Marissa looked especially pretty today, with her glossy dark hair loose and tumbling over her shoulders, those caramel-colored eyes glistening. Her expression seemed shy. Apprehensive? Maybe even sad. It was hard to say, but as she closed the distance between them, she bit down on her bottom lip.

Her scent, something fresh and clean and floral, snaked around him, taunted him, tempting him to put off the conversation they needed to have.

Damn. It was almost as if she already knew what he was going to say, and she was prepared to state her defense. And when it came to putting her best foot forward, she'd pulled out all the stops.

Toughen up, he told himself. *You've got this. Confront her now.*

"Can I talk to you?" she asked. "Alone?"

"Yes. I'd like to talk to you, too. Let's take a walk."

She fell into step beside him, as they followed the pathway that led to Carlene's rose garden, where a cement bench rested under a mulberry tree, flanked by a couple of cherub statues.

They started to talk at the same time, then stopped.

"What did you want to talk to me about?" she asked.

"You first."

She tucked a glossy strand of hair behind her ear, revealing a small pair of earrings. Studs that glinted in the waning light. A golden gem of some kind. Topaz maybe. They looked nice against her olive complexion.

"Okay," she said. "I'm sorry that I was so hesitant when you asked me out to dinner last night."

He now had a pretty good idea why. "I understand."

"No," she said. "I don't think you do. There's something I need to tell you. When I was seventeen, I got arrested for something I didn't do. And no one—not the police, not the attorneys, not the judge and not even my so-called family believed me. I was convicted and served time, a little over a year, and I never even had a single visitor. So I guess you can say that I have trust issues with authority figures." She looked him up and down. "Like cops."

He hadn't seen that coming. But could he believe her? Especially when she claimed no one else had?

"I'm attracted to you," she admitted. "But when I realized you were a law-enforcement officer, I…"

"You didn't want to go out with me."

She nodded. "Yes. But that wasn't fair to you. I shouldn't have judged you based on my experience. I was only seventeen and had to face the criminal-justice system on my own."

"That had to be tough."

"You have no idea how hard it was."

He hoped what she was saying was true. And he wanted to believe her, but… He glanced at the porch, where Maddie giggled at something Jimmy had sketched on his chalkboard.

He had two kids to think about.

"So," Marissa said, her eyes zeroing in on his, "now that you know about my record, you might not want to ask me out again. And I would understand."

"I…I know about your record," he admitted. "About the drugs in your possession and the intention to sell. About your time at the Las Colinas Detention Facility."

Her expression morphed from shy and hopeful to one of surprise and then annoyance. "You already knew? How?"

His cheeks burned, and he shrugged.

"You ran a background check on me?"

"A buddy offered to run it for me, and I didn't stop him."

"Why?"

"I could have accepted the fact that you weren't interested in me. But there was something there. And it seemed like you were almost afraid to go out with me for some reason, and that didn't compute. I had to know why."

Marissa plopped down on the bench, next to a cherub. He'd checked up on her. It was enough to make her want to move far away, to find another place to set down roots. But her past would always come back to haunt her. And Brandon did have two small children to think about, even if there was no way in the world Marissa would be a threat to them.

She supposed he wouldn't know that, though. All he knew so far was whatever legal crap he'd gleaned from his buddy's research. And now her carefully hidden secret, her lousy past, was about to collide with the present. She just hoped it wouldn't knock the bright future she'd planned for herself out of reach.

I had to know why.

"Do you want to hear my side of the story?" she asked. "Because you won't find it in my file."

"If you'd like to tell me."

At this point, she didn't see why not. "My mom died when I was just a baby, so for the first ten years of my life, it was just my dad and me. We were super close, but then he remarried. I actually thought it might be cool to have a mother, like my friends, but it didn't turn out that way. From the day they got home from their honeymoon, it seemed that she and I were always competing for Daddy's attention. Then, two years later, my father died in an industrial accident at work. There was a settlement of some kind, but to this day, I've never seen a penny of it.

"My stepmom became my legal guardian, which wasn't too bad until she remarried a guy who had a son, Erik, who was two years older than me. I never could understand why she seemed to connect more with Erik than she did with me, but he was always kissing up to her, and it worked. I tried to be his friend, but that was a big mistake. He used me. As it turned out, he was a drug dealer. At least, he must have been. That's the only explanation I have for what happened."

"What did he do?" Brandon asked.

"He was a freshman in college, but he lived at home. One day, he invited me to go to a party on campus with him. I was a high-school senior, and I jumped at the chance to hang with him and his friends. Then he told me to get ready and to meet him outside.

"I wanted to make a good impression, so I hurried upstairs, changed clothes and put on some makeup. When I got outside, he told me we'd have to take my car. He wanted me to drive, since he planned on getting high. And heck, I didn't drink anyway, so I agreed.

"When we got there, he spent more time outdoors than he did inside. But I didn't care. People were pretty cool, and I liked learning about college life. After a while, he told me it was time to go. I wasn't ready, but I could tell he'd been drinking. So we left.

"Apparently, the cops got word about drugs going down at that party, and they set up a sobriety checkpoint. I wasn't worried about driving because I'd only been drinking soda pop. But when we rounded the corner and saw the police cars and an officer signaling cars to pull over, Erik jumped out of the passenger seat and ran away. I couldn't go around. I had to go forward, but I wasn't afraid. I hadn't done anything wrong."

She dug her toe in the soft dirt, her gaze on the ground as she relived that night.

"One of the officers had a drug-sniffing dog that started barking at my car. And come to find out, my trunk looked like it belonged to a pharmaceutical sales rep who liked to smoke pot. At the time, I didn't know what the pills were. Later, when I was arrested, I found out it was Ecstasy."

"And Erik never confessed?" Brandon asked, as if he might believe her story when no one else did.

"No. I should have known better than to trust him—or to expect him to come clean before I was officially charged. But no such luck. And for some dumb reason, my stepmom decided to show me tough love so I'd learn my lesson, which meant she refused to bail me out or to pay for a lawyer. I ended up with a public defender who didn't take my claims seriously."

"So you were convicted."

"Yes. And Erik transferred to an out-of-state college, while I went to jail. After I got out, I was sent to a halfway house until I'd finished my probation. Then I moved as far from San Diego as I could."

"And you never contacted them? Your family?"

She chuffed. "No. I kept thinking that someone would try and find me, that they'd apologize and beg for forgiveness. But when that never happened, I wrote them all off and put them and that ugly memory as far away as possible."

She nearly mentioned the texts she'd gotten from Erik, but there was no reason to. It was too late. She wasn't looking for his apology because she wasn't going to forgive him after all this time.

"What about your friends?" Brandon asked. "Didn't they offer you any support?"

"I'd thought they would. But they were all going to college, and most of them had been offered academic scholarships. So they shut me out of their lives after my arrest." And she really couldn't blame them. Who'd want to stay in touch with a convicted criminal, especially when her own family had turned their backs on her?

She slowly shook her head. It was hard to use the word *family* to describe the people she'd once lived with, the people who'd refused to believe or defend her.

Erik's lie had led to her yearlong incarceration and branded her a convicted felon for the rest of her life.

If her daddy had been alive when she'd been falsely convicted of a crime she hadn't committed, he would've moved heaven and earth to help her.

She looked up at Brandon, hoping he would understand. "Do you believe me?" The question came out with a quiver, her voice faint and shaking.

He didn't answer for what seemed like a lifetime. Instead, he studied her as if he was dissecting her story, looking for something that might contradict whatever he'd learned when he'd run that background search.

"I understand." She got to her feet. "I'll stay away from you and your kids. You don't have to worry about me."

Chapter Eight

Did he believe her?

Brandon wasn't entirely sure, but he sure wanted to believe she was telling the truth. Still, the question hung in the air until she got to her feet. He wasn't ready to see her go, so he reached for her hand. "Wait, Marissa. Sit down."

She complied, and they remained in the rose garden for a while, his hand still holding hers.

He'd learned to be skeptical, first when dealing with any excuse one of his irresponsible parents gave him, then when Julie ditched him for her former boyfriend—her so-called soul mate.

And now his job demanded that he question every story, every defense, against hard evidence.

She cleared her throat. "Say something, Brandon."

He turned in his seat, his knee brushing hers and sparking a warmth, even in the chill of the evening.

She gazed at him like a fragile bird. "Do you believe me or not?"

His skepticism faded, and the urge to protect her took its place, whether warranted or not.

"Yes," he said. "I do."

Her shoulders slumped in relief, and she blew out a pent-up sigh. "I was afraid you were going to be like everyone else."

He understood her fear. If what she'd told him was true—and he wanted to believe that it was—she'd only been seventeen and had to face a horrible situation on her own.

"So," she said, "now what?"

He wasn't sure. "Take things slow. See where this goes." Whatever *this* was.

She gave his hand a gentle squeeze before releasing it. "I hoped you'd say that. Do you still want to have that picnic or go out to dinner? If you do, then I'm game. But if not, or if you'd rather wait awhile, I'm okay with that, too."

Once he'd gotten over his initial shock, his gut insisted that she was innocent. That she'd gone through hell without any support from her family or friends. Maybe that's why she'd gravitated toward Alana and the women who lived at Rancho Esperanza. To get the friendship and acceptance she deserved. To find a family, even if they weren't blood-related. To give all that she'd never received.

"I'd still like to go out with you," he said.

"I'm glad to hear that." Her soft, orange-blossom scent stirred in the evening air, surrounding him with wholesome thoughts of goodness. Did that equate to innocence?

"Let's leave the kids out for now and start by having dinner." He didn't want to add them into the mix yet. "Just you and me."

"Okay."

"Does Saturday night work for you?"

She smiled, her eyes sparkling in relief. Or maybe unadulterated hope. "Yes. I'd like that."

"All right, then. I'll pick you up at six."

"I'll be ready."

He was going to suggest that they return to the house, but before he could utter a word, her gaze locked on his. "Your turn. What was it that you had to say to me?"

"We've already talked about it, actually. And I'm glad we did." He turned in the cold, concrete seat, and his knee pressed against hers again, this time sending a spiral of heat through his blood.

Damn, she wasn't just attractive. She looked vulnerable, and he had the strangest compulsion to protect her.

He placed his hand along her jawline, his thumb caressing her cheek. So soft. So... Her lips parted again, and he leaned in to give her a chaste let's-start-over-and-be-friends kiss. At least, that had been his plan until she slipped into his arms, leaned into him and kissed him back.

She had a sweet, lemon-drop taste he found intoxicating. She was intoxicating, and he couldn't seem to get enough of her. He could have kissed her until they were both breathless, but they were too close to the house, and he didn't want the kids to come looking for them and find them in a heated embrace. So he reluctantly ended the kiss.

"I thought you wanted to take things day by day," she said softly, her cheeks flushed.

She was right. And if he dared to kiss her again, he'd be tempted to jump headfirst into the deep end. And if that was to happen, he'd better hope and pray he wasn't making another big mistake in misjudging a woman's character.

Betty Sue sat on the black swivel chair at her favorite slot machine, but her eyes were on the woman Ralph and Carlene had hired to work at the market. There was something about her that didn't seem right. Not that anyone else seemed to notice.

Ella was in her mid-twenties with short jet-black hair—the color that usually came from a bottle. She was of medium height, neither tall nor short, but a little too thin—like a bird. She was skittish like a little sparrow, too. Earlier this morning, Betty accidentally dropped a roll of quarters, and the poor girl nearly jumped a foot.

Sure, some people had quick reactions, but Ella had actually flinched. She also had a tendency to look over her shoulder whenever the door to the store opened. And when she did, she seemed to freeze, and her expression appeared to be more fearful than curious. Betty Sue had no idea what her story was, but she'd bet a nickel to a dollar that it wasn't pretty.

As luck would have it, the Jensen Dairy re-frigerated delivery truck pulled into the yard and parked in back of the market. Carlene and Ralph both left Ella in charge so they could meet with the driver, a man they knew from their high-school days. And Betty Sue took the opportunity to quiz Ella.

She slid off her seat, taking care not to trip, and made her way to the front counter, where the little gal stood near the register. "Do you mind if I ask you a personal question, Ella?"

The poor thing stiffened. "Wh-what's that?"

"Don't worry. You don't have anything to fret about. You're doing a good job. And you're a hard worker. My niece and nephew are pleased that they hired you. But someone I once knew used to move around like you do—always afraid someone might sneak up on her, and I can't help noticing the similarities between her and you."

Ella grew troubled and worried her bottom lip. She stole a glance first at the front door, then at the grocery aisle that led to the back of the market. "I don't know what you're talking about." Then she turned and straightened the packs of cigarettes in the tall glass display case behind the register, which didn't need straightening.

Betty Sue placed a gentle hand on her shoulder. "Who hurt you?"

"I… He…" Tears welled in her eyes, and she used the back of her hand to swipe them away, removing a swatch of makeup in the process and revealing a shiner, albeit one that was fading. "Doug. My husband."

Betty eyed her carefully. "You afraid he'll come looking for you?"

She nodded. "Without a doubt. The last time I left, he swore he'd kill me if I ever tried a stunt like that again."

"Did you call the police?"

"I was afraid to. He's a cop. Or at least, he used to be. He's on a medical leave of absence. But he

has friends on the force. He's also from a prominent family in the community. He told me no one
would believe me, and I knew that was true."

"Cuts and bruises can provide a strong witness.
But at least you're safe now."

"I hope so. I cut my hair short and dyed it. He
probably has no idea where I ended up, but I still
can't help being afraid that he'll figure it out and
find me."

"You have family in Fairborn?"

"No. But he knew how much money I had and
how far the bus would take me. He's mean as
heck, but he's not stupid."

"What does he look like?" Betty Sue asked.

"Doug has brown hair and wears it kind of
short. He's not super tall, but he still looks like
a big man. He played football in college. And he
works out a lot. He's proud of the result and wears
a lot of sleeveless T-shirts. He also drives a red
pickup with gun racks."

Betty Sue eased close to her slowly, in the way
she might have approached a wounded stray dog.
"Do Ralph and Carlene know?"

Ella slowly shook her head. "I was afraid they
wouldn't hire me if they thought there'd be trouble on the horizon."

"I won't say a word," Betty Sue said. "Your
secret is safe with me. But you need to relax. If
you're not careful, your jumpiness is going to set

off alarms. And in case Doug does show up—and I *don't* think he will—someone might say something that could tip him off."

"Thank you for understanding. And for the advice." Tears welled in her eyes again. And she used her fingers to clear them away.

"I'll watch the store. You go on back to the restroom and reapply that makeup. The bruise is a little more prominent now."

"Thanks." She sniffled, then reached for her purse, which she kept under the counter. She started to walk toward the restroom, then paused. "The woman you knew. Was she able to start a new life? Did she stay safe?"

After she shot the bastard. Betty Sue nodded. "She never had to deal with him again."

"And she was your friend?"

"She was me."

Brandon had heard a lot of great things about Feliciano's, the new steak house in Kalispell, which is why he chose to take Marissa there on their first date. But no one had told him about the romantic ambience.

The hostess, a tall brunette in her forties, carried leather-bound menus as she led him and Marissa to their table. They continued past an indoor water fountain, the gurgling sounds drowning out the voices of other diners, and approached a colorful mural of a vineyard on the back wall. Marissa's black heels clicked on the distressed hardwood floor as she walked beside him, her arm brushing against his.

"This place is amazing," she said. "I can see why you didn't want to bring the kids here."

That wasn't his only reason for leaving them with Mrs. Hendrix. Even though she was great with his children, he wanted to get to know Marissa better before he included her in any more family activities.

"You've got that right," he said. "I can imagine Jimmy spilling his milk, and then Maddie scolding him for not being more careful."

"Do they mind staying with a sitter?" she asked.

"Not when it's Mrs. Hendrix. They really like her."

The hostess stopped at a table for two that had been draped with white linen and topped with a flickering candle and a single red rose in a crystal bud vase.

Yet more moving, more stunning, than the setting and atmosphere was his lovely date, who wore a simple, sleeveless black dress and carried a matching wrap. She'd woven her dark locks into a stylish twist that revealed the same yellow-stone studs he'd noticed before.

She looked especially pretty tonight. He'd told

her that when he'd picked her up, but here, in such a romantic setting, she really stood out.

He pulled out her chair, and she thanked him before taking a seat and placing her clutch purse on the table. Then she let her wrap fall from her shoulders behind her. He caught his breath at the sight of her smooth, bronze-colored skin. The soft candlelight cast a magical glow on her lovely face. "Those are pretty earrings."

"Thank you." She fingered her earlobes. "They're topaz. My birthstone. My father gave them to me when I turned twelve."

That must have been right before he died, Brandon thought. Assuming her story was true. But why wouldn't it be?

"That's a nice way to remember your dad."

She smiled. "I think so. I wear them a lot."

Rather than let the conversation slip into something sad or wistful, he changed the subject to a happier one.

"So," he said, "how are the wedding plans coming along?"

"Great." Her warm, brown eyes glimmered in the candlelight, her pride and enthusiasm shining through. "The wedding is next week. The cake is ordered, and so are the flowers. The gazebo is going to be beautiful. And Alana bought the perfect dress. We're only missing one thing. Or rather two."

"What's that?"

"Did Ramon contact you?" she asked.

"Yes." The Fairborn mayor and Brandon were friends and had known each other for years. "Ramon sent me a text and asked if I'd let Jimmy and Maddie take part in the wedding. As the ring bearer and flower girl."

"What did you say?"

"I told him I'd think about it."

Her brow furrowed, and her head tilted slightly to the side. "What's your concern?"

"Actually, I thought it was kind of weird that the twins' names came up. I mean, I really don't know the bride very well. And I only know the groom in a professional capacity." Brandon didn't want her to think Alana's husband had committed a crime, so he added, "Clay was carjacked and assaulted. And I took part in the arrest of the perp."

"Yes, of course."

"Don't Clay and Alana have anyone else that could do it?" he asked. "Like the kids of a friend or family member?"

"Actually, they don't. Do you know Ramon's wife?"

"Of course. Callie."

"She's Alana's best friend and the matron of honor. Alana mentioned that the only thing missing was a ring bearer and flower girl, and when

Callie suggested Jimmy and Maddie, we all thought it was a wonderful idea."

"Ramon and I are pretty tight, so I guess that makes sense."

The waiter, a tall balding man wearing black slacks and a crisply pressed white shirt, stopped by to introduce himself and to take their orders. They decided on a bottle of a Napa Valley merlot to start and the chateaubriand for two. Once he'd walked away from the table, Marissa leaned forward. "So what do you say? Can the kids be in the wedding?" She paused. "I'm sorry. Am I being too pushy? I don't want you to do something you're uncomfortable with."

If his agreement would keep her smiling for the rest of the evening, how could he say no? Besides, he knew how important the wedding plans were to her. So he said, "All right."

"Great. I assume you got your invitation?"

"I did," Brandon said. It was a small town, and people usually included everyone.

"Good. And with the twins in the ceremony, you should attend the rehearsal dinner the night before. But just so you know, having the kids take part won't cost you anything. Clay will pay to rent a little tuxedo for Jimmy, so all you'd need to do is take Jimmy to the Tux Shop and have him measured—and the sooner the better. Clay is also going to buy Maddie's dress. I've already picked out the perfect little gown. I'm sure a size four will fit her. If not, we can have it altered."

Brandon didn't like other people picking up the tab for him or his children. "I'll pay for the dress and tux."

"You really don't have to. Clay was prepared to spend a fortune on the wedding, although Alana insisted upon keeping it simple. And for the most part, that's the plan. It'll be an outdoor event with a country theme. And really, your kids are going to look so cute."

Marissa definitely had things all planned out, but Brandon knew things rarely went the way he expected, especially when it came to his children. "I have to warn you, Jimmy isn't keen on baths or dressing up. But if a fancy dress is involved, Maddie will be all over it. She's really into all things royal these days, so she'll be thrilled to wear what she's going to consider a princess costume."

"Then, maybe I'd better look for a small tiara she can wear, although I was thinking a headband made of real flowers." She lifted her finger, the nail painted pink, and tapped her chin, as if her creative brain was working hard to figure it out.

Brandon couldn't help smiling. "Maddie will be happy either way."

"I'm sure she will, but I want everything to be perfect." Marissa took a deep breath, then slowly let it out. "I think I have everything under control, but there's just one thing that might go wrong."

"What's that?"

"Callie is eight months pregnant and expecting twins. The doctor thinks she will go into labor anytime. I just hope it doesn't happen before next Saturday. Or during the wedding. Can you imagine?"

"That would be a complication." But that wasn't the only thing that could go wrong. Jimmy could lose the ring. Or accidentally knock over the cake. And Maddie could trip on her way down the aisle and burst into tears…

He glanced at the happy wedding planner. Hopefully, she'd still be happy after the ceremony, no matter what went south. Because with his twins involved, anything could go wrong.

As Marissa and Brandon left the restaurant and headed toward his Jeep, she said, "Thank you for a lovely evening. The food was to die for. And the candles and roses, that amazing fountain, the excellent service. I've never been to such a nice restaurant before. Except once." She touched her earrings. "When my dad gave these to me, he took me to a fancy restaurant on the top floor of a building that looked out over San Diego. It was for brunch, and I still remember I had pancakes and fruit salad."

"I'm glad you enjoyed it."

She really had, so much so that she wished the night would never end, but he had children at home. And a babysitter to relieve.

He opened the passenger door for her, and she slid onto the seat. Then he circled the car and got behind the wheel.

Once he started the engine, backed out of the parking space and pulled onto the street, she said, "Tell me about Mrs. Hendrix. And why do the kids like her so much?"

"She's our neighbor—and a widow. Her kids live out of state, and they're building careers. They haven't started families yet, so she's kind of adopted Jimmy and Maddie. Whenever she bakes cookies, she always brings some to us."

"They're lucky," Marissa said, wishing she'd had a grandmotherly neighbor or someone who'd taken an interest in her when she'd been a child.

"And Mrs. Hendrix is lucky to have them, too. She's going to start watching them on the days they're not in preschool and when I'm on duty. She didn't want me to pay her, but I told her that's the only way I'd agree to the arrangement." He chuckled. "She said I drove a hard bargain."

"So they won't be staying with Carlene and Ralph anymore?"

"No," he said. "I'm trying to give my aunt and uncle a bit of a break."

"Are the kids too much for them?"

"They said no, but they're getting older, and they refuse to retire. They have a lot of responsibilities with the store. And they admit that Betty Sue and the twins keep them busy. We'll still visit them regularly. Only now they won't have to worry about messes and discipline."

"I'm glad they'll still get to spend time with you and the kids."

"Me, too. I'd like to see them take a vacation someday. In fact, they finally hired a part-time employee to help at the market. I hope that works out for them."

He was talking about Ella. Marissa nearly told him that she'd been instrumental in making the introductions, but she didn't want to come across as prideful or tooting her own horn. She'd rather earn Brandon's trust and respect by being herself and not for what she may or may not have done for his family.

As Brandon turned onto the country road that would take Marissa back to Rancho Esperanza, he said, "And believe it or not, Betty Sue can be pretty fussy at times. But she seems to like the woman they hired. That'll be helpful since Carlene and Ralph will probably ask her to keep an eye on Betty Sue once in a while. Don't get me wrong. I love my great-aunt, but she can be a handful sometimes."

"I'm glad things are working out for everyone involved." She was also happy to know that she'd helped Ella create a new start, a better life and a safer environment.

"I haven't met the woman yet, but my aunt and uncle assured me that she's been very helpful and that she tries hard." Brandon cut a glance across the seat. "By the way, what's the dress code for that wedding?"

"You can wear a jacket if you want to, but slacks and a button-down shirt should be okay. I'll be wearing a dress, of course. And working behind the scenes."

"Good to know."

They continued to chat for the rest of the twenty-minute ride about nothing in particular and everything in general. The dashboard lights lit his face, and Marissa liked the way his eyes crinkled at the corners when he smiled.

"Was it hard to return to town after college? With the twins and no wife?"

He shrugged. "I wasn't embarrassed by it, if that's what you mean. And my family was great. I don't know what I would have done without my aunt and uncle."

Marissa remained quiet for a while, happy for him. It must be nice to have a loving, accepting family. Her life certainly would have been a lot easier if she'd had someone to lean on, someone who'd loved her.

As Brandon turned into the long driveway that led to the ranch house, ending the memorable evening, Marissa again thanked him.

"You're welcome. I'm glad you went with me to check out Feliciano's. That's not the kind of place a guy would want to go alone."

Maybe not, but Brandon wouldn't have had any trouble finding another woman to date. He had to be one of the most eligible bachelors in the county. And she was happy that he'd chosen her. She was also relieved to know that he believed in her innocence, that he believed in *her*.

He parked, and as she opened the passenger door, he got out of the Jeep, too. Then they walked together to the porch, where an outdoor light bathed them in a soft, yellow glow.

Would he kiss her again? She hoped he would. Ever since the last time, she'd been thinking and dreaming about it. She paused before the screen door, but it seemed silly to thank him yet again, so she said, "I guess I'll see you at the rehearsal dinner. Friday, at six o'clock. At the ranch."

"Yes, I'll see you then. If not before."

Then he kissed her, slowly at first. Sweetly. But as his woodsy scent caressed her, she reached up and slipped her arms around his neck and kissed him back—full throttle.

Her lips parted, allowing his tongue to seek hers, to meet and mate. Their hands stroked, caressed and explored each other, the fabric of his shirt and her dress preventing any skin-to-skin contact. If she didn't live with a houseful of people, she'd be tempted to invite him inside for coffee, a nightcap or...whatever. But it probably wouldn't be very wise for her to do, anyway.

So she reluctantly lowered her arms and withdrew her mouth from his.

"Damn," he said. "That was one hot good-night kiss."

Ditto, she thought. The sparks of heat darn near lit up the night sky.

"I'll talk to you later," he said.

"Sounds good." She had no idea what he meant by *later*, but she certainly hoped it was soon. And before the rehearsal dinner.

Chapter Nine

As it turned out, Marissa didn't see Brandon that next week, which had been a little disappointing, but she'd kept busy with the wedding plans.

By the time Friday rolled around, the evening before the wedding, the party-rental company had made their delivery. They'd set up the chairs the way Marissa had instructed, with an aisle down the middle, in front of the new white gazebo, which had turned out beautifully, even though it hadn't been decorated yet. The florist would bring the flowers and greenery tomorrow morning. But for now, everything was ready for the wedding party, who'd be coming soon.

As the sun dipped low in the western sky, Marissa stood in the yard, making one final assessment for tonight's event. Two large tables sat at the side of the house on the lawn. In keeping with Alana and Clay's country-wedding theme, each had been adorned with yellow tablecloths and multiple bouquets of wildflowers arranged in quart-size mason jars, each trimmed with multi-colored ribbons. Mini-lanterns and string lights crisscrossed above the tables, providing romantic lighting.

Pleased with the setup, Marissa returned to the kitchen, where Ella had been cooking up a storm, the results filling the house with the aroma of savory beef, roasting vegetables and herbs. The first whiff reminded her of the restaurant Brandon had taken her to last week, high-end and outrageously delicious.

Their new roommate hadn't lived on the ranch for a full twenty-four hours when they learned that she was a whiz at cooking—and not just for small groups. So even though Clay had offered to hire a catering company to provide the wedding meal, he and Alana had asked Ella to prepare tonight's rehearsal dinner. She wasn't going to accept payment, but Clay insisted.

Marissa made her way to the counter, where Ella was placing plastic wrap over the top of the salad bowl. "That looks amazing. What all did you put in it?"

"Besides the greens? There's goat cheese, toasted walnuts, pumpkin seeds and figs." Ella smiled proudly. "Plus my secret homemade dressing, which is already in the fridge."

In addition to that yummy salad and roasted veggies, tonight's menu would also consist of a choice of petite filets of beef with a balsamic demi-glace and breast of chicken sautéed in marsala wine sauce, with an option for the vegetarians—pumpkin and butternut-squash ravioli. Dessert would be make-it-yourself ice-cream sundaes.

Tomorrow, a caterer would show up with a specialized chuck wagon, where he would grill Santa Maria–style tri tip on-site. To go with it, Ella would make red potatoes and a southwestern green salad with another of her secret dressings.

"Everything smells so good," Marissa said. "I knew the meals would be delicious, but where did you learn to balance out all the kitchen chores like this?"

"My grandmother used to be a caterer, and when I was a teenager, she let me help."

"She certainly taught you a lot." Marissa glanced at the luscious fruit salad that filled a large hollowed-out watermelon that had been carved to look like a fancy basket.

"I'm also addicted to the Food Network,"

Ella added. "I would've loved to attend culinary school, but… Well, I got married, and then my life plans sort of stalled." She fingered a fading bruise on her neck. With a nervous laugh, she added, "Then it went into a tailspin."

"Well, you're safe now," Marissa said. "It's time to make your happiness a priority. You can still go to school—if you want to."

"Maybe." Ella shrugged. "Wouldn't that be something?"

"Yes. Something you absolutely can do." Marissa glanced at the clock on the oven. The pastor and his wife would be arriving soon. Clay's father, Mr. Hastings, too. Her heartbeat skipped. And Brandon.

"Did you do anything special for the kids?" Marissa asked. "I should have asked their father if they were fussy eaters."

"I have some chicken tenders and macaroni and cheese on hand. So if they don't want an adult meal, it won't be a problem."

"Perfect. I'll check with Brandon as soon as he arrives." Marissa scanned the kitchen, which was surprisingly tidy. "Is there anything I can do to help?"

"Not that I can think of. I've got everything under control. And the table settings are gorgeous."

And that meant that—so far, and fingers

crossed—Marissa had the entire evening under control. She began mentally checking off her last-minute to-do list. Hmm. "Maybe I should make seating assignments."

"I don't think that's necessary. There's not that many people coming."

"You're probably right. I have both tables side by side and set them for twelve."

"Isn't that too many?" Ella asked. "I made enough food, but I didn't think either of Clay's brothers would be arriving from Texas until tomorrow."

"Let's see." Marissa began counting them off. "There's the bride and groom, matron of honor and best man. Then there's Mr. Hastings. Pastor Jennings and his wife. Brandon and the twins. You and me. That makes twelve."

"I won't be joining you guys for the rehearsal or the dinner. I'll just serve the meals and then come back to the kitchen and clean up."

Marissa was about to object, to insist that Ella join them, but the doorbell rang, and she hurried to greet the first arrivals. It might be the pastor and his wife. Or maybe Callie and Ramon. But it could just as easily be Brandon and the kids, who she was most eager to see. So she kicked up her pace as she crossed the living room. When she opened the door and spotted Brandon and the twins standing on the stoop, her heart took a tumble, and a warm smile stretched across her face. "Come on in, guys. I'm so glad you're here."

She stepped aside, and as the kids entered the living room, Marissa's eyes locked on the gorgeous daddy. The deputy looked incredibly nice tonight in a pair of black jeans and a white button-down shirt. He smelled good, too.

He stepped through the door, the scent of soap and a masculine cologne trailing behind him, setting her senses on high alert.

"I never got to go to a wedding before," Maddie said, drawing Marissa's attention. "Daddy said I get to be the flower girl and wear a princess dress."

"Yeah," Jimmy said. "And I get to be the ring boy."

"Can I wear the dress now?" Maddie asked.

Marissa's heart melted. What a sweet *ring boy* and flower girl.

"I'll let you see the dress, but you'll need to wait until tomorrow to wear it. You'll even get to take it home with you."

Clearly disappointed, the little girl scrunched her face.

Before Marissa could show her the child-size gown, the doorbell sounded.

"I'd better get that," she said. It was probably the minister and his wife.

Instead, it was Adam Hastings, Clay's father. Marissa invited him in.

Mr. Hastings wasn't a tall man, but the wealthy Texas rancher carried himself in a way that commanded respect. He removed his cowboy hat when he entered. "You must be the wedding planner."

A sense of pride settled over her, and she offered the older man a smile. "Yes, I am. Marissa Garcia. Please come in and make yourself comfortable."

She'd no more than closed the door when she heard footsteps approaching from down the hall. She looked over her shoulder to see Clay and Alana, who'd been talking privately in the ranch office. She had no idea what they'd been discussing, but it must have been something happy because they were all smiles.

Marissa had hardly taken a breath, when the matron of honor and the best man arrived. Callie had a healthy glow as she waddled inside, her husband, Ramon, at her side.

Moments later, the pastor and his wife entered the house, and the rehearsal was on.

So much for having any time to spend with Brandon and his sweet son and daughter. And tomorrow would be another busy day. But that didn't matter. Marissa had planned the perfect wedding, and if everything went as it was supposed to, she'd be one step closer to opening White Lace and Promises.

The rehearsal had been a success, and Saturday dawned bright and warm. Marissa couldn't be happier with the way Alana and Clay's wedding had come together. The gazebo, now adorned in greenery and an array of colorful blooms, most of them sunflowers, sat in front of a copse of weeping willows. A pond to the side provided a lovely view of the countryside.

Rows of rented white chairs flanked a white carpeted aisle the bridal party would walk down. And the guests would start arriving soon.

With Alana marrying an attorney whose family had more money than they knew what to do with, they could have pulled out all the stops in planning their ceremony, even though they had a baby on the way and had opted to marry quickly. Clay's father had wanted to invite hundreds of his friends and associates, which both the bride and groom nixed. From what Marissa had heard, Adam Hastings was used to getting his way, so the fact that he'd pretty much folded on the idea said a lot about his willingness to build a better, more respectful relationship with his youngest son.

"Marissa!"

She turned at the sound of the child's voice and

spotted the adorable little red-haired girl dressed in a princess-style gown and her dapper twin brother rocking a little tuxedo and tugging at his bow tie. A smile that began in her heart spread across her face as she started toward them, her gaze bursting with appreciation for the flower girl and the ring boy, not to mention the daddy who'd done his best to get them ready.

"Maddie, you look beautiful—a perfect little princess. And, Jimmy, aren't you handsome in that grown-up suit and tie."

The girl beamed, while her brother scrunched his face. "Do I have to wear this thing? Bows are for girls."

"Maybe, if it's okay with your dad, you can take if off after the ceremony." Marissa turned to the handsome daddy, who wore a pair of black slacks, a pale blue button-down shirt and a smile that nearly stole her breath away. She preferred the deputy in civilian clothes, either casual or dressy. But she had to admit, even in his uniform, he looked nice.

Brandon placed his hand on Jimmy's small shoulder. "I'd agree with that. You can ditch the tie after the wedding." He scanned the parking lot. "My uncle and aunts are coming, but I haven't seen them yet."

Marissa glanced toward the area they'd set

aside as a parking lot. "There's a shiny new pickup. Isn't that him now?"

"Yes, that's him. He loves that truck. He has a friend who now works at the dealership, and he got a good deal."

"Who wouldn't love a deal like that?" Marissa scanned the grounds, checking out the gazebo, the caterers setting up the tables, the pastor wiping his brow with a white handkerchief. She wasn't wearing a watch, but the clock was ticking. "I'd love to hang with you guys a little longer, but I need to go inside and check on the bride and her matron of honor."

"Do what you need to do." Brandon flashed her a smile. "Now that it's getting down to the wire, you've got your work cut out for you. And so do I." He nodded toward the twins. "I need to keep these two little munchkins clean and presentable for the next twenty minutes."

What a good daddy. And a wonderful man. She took one last moment to admire the handsome deputy she'd come to trust. With all the love and romance in the air today, it'd be in her best interest to do her job and keep her mind on the couple who'd soon be tying the knot.

Still, when she approached the French doors at the back end of the house that led to the master bedroom, she stole one last glance over her shoulder at Brandon. He stood near the gazebo, where a few women had already gathered around him, fawning over the kids. And clearly fawning over him, too.

A pang of jealousy hit, and she did her best to tamp it down. She had no reason to feel the least bit possessive. Not yet, anyway. But the way things seemed to be going, maybe it was just a matter of time.

When Carlene and Ralph stopped to talk to Eddie Cruz, Ramon's father, and his date—Helena Somebody-or-other—Betty Sue took the opportunity to slip away and head to the small orchard, where she plucked some ripe cherries from the tree and stashed them in her purse to eat later. She'd attended plenty of weddings in her day, although never her own. But very few of them served a meal on time.

As she headed back to the festivities, where people were beginning to take their seats, she scanned the small crowd, looking for Ella. The other day, at the market, Ella had mentioned that she was preparing tonight's food. Poor thing was probably slaving in the kitchen. Betty Sue had promised to look out for her, and she'd meant it. Even if that meant washing dishes or serving meals.

So she circled the ranch house, like some of the later arrivals, and entered through the back door.

She spotted the frail little thing in the kitchen, wearing a white, full-length apron and peering out the kitchen window and into the yard.

"What are you doing holed up in here?" Betty Sue asked.

Ella jumped, spun around and slapped a hand over her chest. "Oh, my gosh! You startled me."

With her black hair too dark against her fair skin, the short strands poking up like she'd stuck her finger in an electrical outlet, she looked scared to death. "Why aren't you outside with the others? I can see that you'd like to be out there."

Ella slowly shook her head. "I might be a little curious, but I'd rather stay inside. Weddings make me uneasy."

"Why's that?"

She shrugged. "My marriage was a nightmare. But it's over now. Well, it will be, once I can get a legal divorce. And that's not likely to happen anytime soon. There's no way I'd want Doug to find out where I am."

"I hear you."

Betty Sue eased forward and checked out the dessert tray Ella was filling with a variety of sweet treats—tiny little pies and cakes a person could eat in a single bite. "Did you make this fussy stuff for your husband?"

"No way. I tried it once, and he threw every single one of them at me. He's a meat-and-potatoes sort of guy. His favorite after-dinner treat was a twelve-pack of beer."

Booze and drugs could make a macho man mean as hell. They could also make him ugly.

"Don't you like to cook?" Ella asked.

"I used to. I even worked at a natural-food store once. In the bakery. But I got fired."

"Oh, no." Ella sobered. "What happened?"

"My special brownie recipe had always gone over big. I called them Brownie Boosters. So I whipped up a batch at home one day and took them to the store to see how the customers would like them."

"I'm sure the store owner was concerned about health regulations."

Betty Sue lifted her hand and waved her off. "That wasn't the problem. Hell, people couldn't get enough of them, although I had to sell them under the counter."

Ella's eyebrows rose, and her eyes grew wide. "Brownie *Boosters*? You mean, you put marijuana in them?"

Betty Sue nodded proudly.

Ella chuckled. "And I thought you were a sweet old lady."

"Honey, you have no idea how sweet I am. I'm also very resourceful. Anyway, when word got out, the bakery's sales and profits shot through the roof."

"So the owner got a cut?"

"Of course. I'm no thief."

"Then, why did you get fired?"

"One Sunday morning before church, Pastor Babbitt stopped in the store and ordered a bagful. He'd always had a sweet tooth. I suspect he ate them all, because mid-sermon the boost hit him. He'd just launched into the fire-and-brimstone part when he got the giggles and couldn't stop." Betty Sue smirked and folded her arms across her chest. "I'm not a churchgoer, so I wasn't there. But folks said he wrapped up the sermon and said, 'Let's start the potluck. I'm starving.'"

Ella placed a hand over her mouth to staunch her laughter. "You're funny."

"Maybe so. And you're not the only one who's mentioned it. Too bad my family can't connect with my sense of humor."

Ella's expression turned serious. "Tell me something. When we were talking at the market the other day, you said that you'd been abused, too. But the minute Carlene returned from the back room, you dropped the subject. That was okay with me, because I didn't want her to learn about my situation, either. I like my job and the Tiptons. And I don't want to give them any reason to fire me."

"I kept my beatings quiet, too," Betty Sue said. "Ashamed, I guess. But at least I wasn't married to my abuser. 'Course, that didn't mean there weren't legal repercussions. And a trial."

"Do you mind telling me about it?" Ella asked.

If Betty Sue was going to talk to anyone about that day back in 1968—August the fourth, to be exact—it would be the shy kid hanging on her every word. She glanced at the doorway that led to the front part of the house, as well as the doorway to the mudroom. A glance out the kitchen window let her know that the guests had begun to take their seats.

"I'd better tell you later," Betty Sue said. "Carlene will be calling 9-1-1 if I don't get out there and take my seat. But I swore I'd never let anyone lay a hand on me again."

"Thanks for being my friend." Ella closed the distance between them and gave Betty Sue a hug that damn near knocked her to her knees, as scarred and arthritic as they were.

It was the first adult-size hug Betty Sue had been given in ages, and it made her tear up. Still, she held Ella tight, stroking her back, the bony vertebrae revealing just how thin the poor kid was. Who would have guessed that this frail, frightened little gal would be the first real friend she'd had in a long, long time?

Alana was the epitome of the blushing bride, yet even the pink tint on her olive complexion looked as if it had been professionally applied by an experienced makeup artist. And her dress was perfect: ivory-colored, knee-length, with a sweetheart-lace bodice, a scoop neck and elbow-length sleeves. Her baby bump refused to hide under the material that gathered under her bust-line. It was almost as if her son, who wouldn't arrive for another three months, was determined to take part in the wedding that would join his happy parents in marriage.

Callie, the matron of honor, was just as lovely in a similarly styled maternity dress. Her light brown hair had been swept up in a bun, adorned with a crown of yellow roses to match her dress. She looked a little uncomfortable, though. But who wouldn't be? She was about to have twins, and those active little ones had stretched the soft, jersey-like fabric around her belly.

While the bride and her matron of honor did a last-minute makeup check, Marissa couldn't help but stand beside the two pregnant friends, marveling at how close they were, how supportive they were of each other.

The two women had been friends ever since they met as teenagers. And while Marissa was happy for them, she couldn't help feeling a wee bit envious. Maybe, one of these days, she would have her very own BFF.

"You both look beautiful," Marissa said.

"Should I let the pastor know that we're ready to start the ceremony?"

"Yes, we're ready." Alana gave Callie a warm hug. "Let's do this."

As Marissa turned to leave, she'd barely taken two steps toward the door when Callie cried out, "Uh-oh."

Alana let out a loud gasp, and Marissa spun around to see both women staring at Callie's high heels and a puddle on the floor.

Marissa's eyes widened, and she pointed. "Is that…?"

Callie nodded. "I'm afraid so. My water broke."

Too stunned to speak, let alone move, Marissa's mind began spinning a mile a minute as she tried to make sense of what had happened. What it meant.

What would a seasoned wedding planner do at a time like this?

Her first thought was to ask the pastor to speed up the ceremony, but that wouldn't work. Callie was expecting twins, and anything could go wrong at this point.

"Will you please get my husband?" Callie said.

"Yes. Of course." Marissa hurried out the bedroom door. The last time she checked on the groom and his best man, they'd been downing a beer in the guest room down the hall.

She knocked at the door, then opened it and entered without waiting for an invitation. Both men stopped chuckling at whatever they'd been talking about.

"We've got a problem," she said.

Clay got to his feet. "Don't tell me my father is barking out orders again. Dammit. We talked about that, and he promised—"

"No, he's fine. A perfect gentleman." She turned to Ramon, who appeared to be kicking back until their gazes met. "Callie's in labor. Her water just broke."

The new mayor jumped to his feet. "Oh, man. Is she okay?"

"Yes. I mean, so far. But—"

"I'm on it." Ramon turned to Clay. "I'm sorry, man. I hate to leave at a time like this, but the doctor told us not to drag our feet if something like this happened. She's already dilated, and one baby wasn't in an optimum position."

"Go," Clay said. "But drive carefully."

Ramon tossed him an unsteady grin. "Don't worry. I will. I've got precious cargo on board."

As he dashed off, Marissa crossed her arms and blew out a sigh. "I know you're not supposed to see the bride before the ceremony, but maybe we ought to make an exception in this case. I'd like to know if you guys want to proceed with just the two of you, postpone things or—"

Clay shook his head. "Alana won't want to postpone the ceremony. And I don't, either. Let's talk to her and see what she has to say. I want this day to be perfect for her."

"It'll definitely be memorable."

Five minutes later, Marissa went outside, where Brandon stood with the twins, attempting to keep them in line until they got the cue to start the walk down the aisle.

Maddie, a basket of flower petals in her hand, spotted Marissa first. "Is it time yet?"

"Yeah," Jimmy said. "I want to take off my bow. And I can't do it until after that man and lady kiss."

Rather than answer the twins, Marissa turned to their daddy, who was probably ready to get this show on the road, too. "I'm afraid there's a problem. Not a bad one. A joyful one. Sort of. I'm sure everything will be okay…" She was rambling, and she knew it.

"What's going on?" he asked.

"Callie's water just broke, and Ramon has taken her to the hospital."

"Wow." Brandon combed his hand through his hair, leaving it looking stylishly mussed instead of military crisp.

"Did she get cut really bad?" Jimmy asked. "When the glass broke and she spilled the water?"

Marissa placed a hand on his head. "No, honey. She didn't get cut. She's going to the hospital because it's time for her to have her babies."

Brandon blew out a sigh. "Is there something I can do?"

"Actually, there is."

"I'm not on duty, but I can call the substation and get them a police escort."

"I think Ramon beat you to that." She took a deep, fortifying breath. "We need a stand-in for the best man."

Brandon furrowed his brow. "Surely you don't mean *me*?"

"Yes, I do. I'm going to cover for Callie. And Ramon has already handled all the best man duties. So all you have to do is stand next to Clay at the gazebo and look supportive and happy for him."

"I *am* happy for him, but what about one of Clay's Texas friends? Or even one of the other attorneys in his firm? Hell, he's got two brothers here. Why not ask one of them?"

"I suggested those alternatives, too. But Clay wanted to keep the wedding fairly small, so he didn't invite any of his friends. And he was in private practice, so he doesn't have any coworkers. On top of that, he isn't very close to either of his brothers and, even if he was, he doesn't want to choose one over the other. He'd prefer to have a local friend."

Brandon couldn't hide his disbelief. "But I'm *not* a friend."

"Not yet. But he's a great guy. And now that he and Alana own the neighboring ranch, he's a big landowner in town. I'm sure you'll be friends before you know it. So what do you say?"

Brandon had no idea what to say, but he knew how important this event was to her. And they'd just lost the best man and the matron of honor in one fell swoop. But if the wedding was a success in spite of that, word would spread in the community, and she'd earn a name for herself as a wedding planner.

He glanced down at the twins, who were gazing at him as if he had all the answers. He looked at the anxious wedding planner, then checked his wristwatch. "The ceremony should be taking place right now. I'm not dressed appropriately, and it's too late for me to find a tux."

"You look fine. Nice. Perfect."

A guitar sounded from the gazebo, where the pastor's wife sat off to the side, providing soft music.

Brandon let out a sigh. He guessed he'd have to take one for the team. "What do I have to do?" he asked.

"You attended the rehearsal last night. So all you need to do is to join Clay inside the house. The two of you will stroll out to the gazebo together. I'll take the twins inside and tell Alana it's time to walk down the aisle. Then I'll pick up Callie's bouquet, and the rest will go on as planned."

And she was right. Minutes later, Clay had loaned Brandon a black bolo tie. And now they both stood in front of the gazebo, to the left of the Pastor Jennings, a tall, jovial young minister in his early thirties.

As Maddie and Jimmy walked down the aisle, just like they'd practiced last night, Brandon damn near popped a button on his white shirt, even though Maddie was dropping clumps of flower petals instead of tossing them lightly, and the satin pillow Jimmy held listed to the side. Fortunately someone had tied the ring on top.

Marissa followed the twins, smiling as if she didn't have a care in the world. But heck, why shouldn't she be happy? She'd just handled her first mishap, and no one outside of the wedding party was the wiser.

She looked lovely today in a summery sundress with a pale green background and a floral print. Her hair was swept up in an intricate twist, revealing two sparkling studs—the topaz gemstones her father had given her. She whispered a silent thank-you to Brandon when she reached the front.

He might have continued to gawk at her, but Stacy, Pastor Jennings's wife, got to her feet and struck a different guitar chord, alerting the crowd that the bride was coming. Instead of the traditional wedding march, she played "Forever and Ever, Amen," a classic country tune made popular by Randy Travis.

Adam Hastings walked Alana down the aisle, and the ceremony began.

Moments later, after Pastor Jennings pronounced Clay and Alana husband and wife, they kissed—sweetly, lovingly and with the promise of a long and happy life together. Then they proceeded down the aisle. Brandon offered Marissa his arm, and she took it. As they followed the bride and groom, it took all he had not to glance over his shoulder to make sure Maddie and Jimmy were taking up the rear, just as they'd practiced.

They'd no more than reached the last row of chairs when Jimmy let out a happy shriek. "Whoo-hoo! We did it! Daddy and Marissa got married, too."

The wedding guests burst into laughs and giggles. And Brandon merely shook his head. He never knew what one of his youngsters was going to say next. He'd have to correct that misunderstanding before the Fairborn rumor mill kicked into high gear.

But with all the excitement, not to mention the love in the air, he couldn't help having a few romantic thoughts of his own. He turned to Marissa, her fingers still holding his arm, and smiled. "Do you have plans for tomorrow?"

"What do you have in mind?" she asked.

"How about a picnic at the park. With the kids."

Her golden-brown eyes lit up, and a smile spread across her pretty face, dimpling her cheeks. "I'd love that."

So would Brandon.

Chapter Ten

The wedding had gone off without a hitch, other than the mad dash Ramon and Callie had made to the hospital. By the time the cake had been cut, Ramon called to let Alana know that his and Callie's newborns had arrived, and that mama and babies were doing great. Talk about happy endings! And new beginnings, Brandon thought the next afternoon, as he and Marissa watched Maddie and Jimmy play at the park. A warm, bright sun and a cool breeze made it a perfect day for a picnic. He would have picked up hamburgers or a pizza, but Marissa had insisted on making their lunch: turkey sandwiches for the adults and peanut butter and jelly for the kids. She'd also packed a thermos of iced tea, juice boxes, fruit slices and homemade chocolate-chip cookies for dessert.

Maddie and Jimmy had played for a while, eaten lunch and then run back to the playground, where they were now taking turns going up and down the slide.

Brandon stole a glance at Marissa, who sat beside him on a blanket she'd spread on the grass. She wore a red top and a pair of white shorts that revealed shapely, tanned legs. Yet it was the expression on her pretty face that caught his rapt attention, the delight she seemed to take in watching his children play. Then her smile faded, and she turned to him.

The breeze whipped a couple strands of dark hair across her eyes, and she brushed them aside. "Alana and Clay will be in Hawaii for the next two weeks. While they're gone, would you mind if I invited Jimmy and Maddie to spend a day with me at the ranch? I could show them the horses, dogs and chickens. And maybe we could make cookies."

She wanted to spend the day with the twins? She hadn't included him, so the question surprised him, and he didn't immediately respond.

"If you're not ready for something like that," she said, "I understand. And we don't need to set a date. Maybe sometime. I mean, in the future."

"Sure. Someday. If you're sure they won't be too much for you."

"Seriously? I'd really enjoy having them around. We could play games. And color pictures. Whatever."

"They'd probably like that," he said.

She nodded, then returned her gaze to the playground, where Maddie and Jimmy had moved from the slide to a dome-shaped jungle gym, but her expression remained pensive. He was tempted to say something that might draw another wistful smile. But before he could come up with something, she turned to him and asked, "Are the kids ever too much for you?"

"I must admit, when they were babies, it wasn't easy, and I hardly slept. And even now, they can be a handful at times. They really keep me hopping, especially with all their questions. But I can't imagine what my life would be without them."

"Lonely, I suppose."

"You got that right." He shot another glance her way, wondering if maybe she was lonely at times, if that's what she'd been thinking about. Growing up without a sibling. Losing her father. Facing the criminal-justice system on her own.

At times, he supposed, he was lonely, too. Not that he didn't have a loving family. He stole another look at Marissa. What would his life be like if she were to become a part of it, even just a small part?

"Will you tell me about their mother?" she asked.

He hadn't been prepared to talk about Julie. And most people, other than his family, had never asked.

"I don't mean to be nosy," Marissa added. "I just…wondered about her."

"She was a fine-arts major. I met her after my return to college. I'd just changed my major from business to criminal justice." It had been a better fit for a guy who had a protective streak and who believed in truth and justice.

"Did you love her?" Marissa asked. "I guess that's pretty obvious that you did."

"I thought so. But in retrospect, it was lust." And on both of their parts. The beautiful, sexy, blonde city girl had swept him off his cowboy boots. "When she got pregnant, I offered to marry her, but she refused. I stuck by her during her pregnancy and was at the hospital when the twins were born."

"You're a wonderful father."

He shrugged. "I try to be."

"You really are. I've seen you interact with them. I suspect that on your worst day, you're better than most parents on their best."

He hoped so. "Thanks for the vote of confidence."

"It's hard to imagine you, as a college student, raising two newborns on your own."

"Julie was more involved back then. At first, anyway. And I tried to do my best to help her—and not just financially. I watched the babies for her whenever she was in class. In fact, after a while, I realized that I had them more often than she did." Damn, he loved those kids. Even when they were crying and he couldn't figure out why. Walking the floor with them. Talking to tiny babies who didn't understand a word he said but seemed to feel what was in his heart. "I could never understand why she wasn't as attached to them as I was."

He shot another glance at Marissa, saw the way she'd scrunched her brow in thought. "Does she come around to see them? To visit?"

"No, she's not involved with them at all." He still found it hard to believe Julie could just walk away from her babies the way she had. "Right before their first birthday, she told me she'd hooked up with an old boyfriend, a guy who'd spent time in jail and had just been released."

"That must have been a tough blow," Marissa said, her tone soft, compassionate. Yet her brow remained furrowed, her demeanor pensive.

"My aunt and uncle believed children needed

both a mother and a father. I agreed, at least in theory. But in this case, I knew what my children didn't need. And that was a stepfather prone to criminal behavior."

Marissa nodded her agreement.

Still, Brandon hadn't meant to dwell on the past, to spill his guts like that. So he changed the subject. "Hey, did you hear they're opening up a new organic grocery in town?"

"Oh, really?"

Before either of them could continue the small talk, the twins ran up and asked if they could have another cookie. Marissa looked at Brandon, waiting for his approval.

"Sure," he said.

Marissa reached into the basket she'd brought and passed out two more cookies, and the kids dashed off. But for the rest of the afternoon, she remained fairly quiet. He supposed she was probably thinking about Julie, about the relationship they'd had, the way it had ended. And to be honest, the past was weighing on his mind, too.

Thankfully, Marissa hadn't let her pensive mood affect her interactions with Jimmy and Maddie. She continued to answer their questions and be attentive to their chatter. So he didn't let the fact that she'd clammed up when it came to their adult interactions bother him too much.

At least, when it did, he didn't let it show.

* * *

Marissa spent a lonely evening by herself at the ranch. With Alana and Clay on their honeymoon, the house was quiet. Even Ella, who'd moved in a couple of weeks ago, was either working or visiting a friend, although Marissa wasn't sure who it was. Just that it was someone she'd met at the market.

And since Katie Johnson, the young college student who lived in one of the outbuildings with her two younger brothers, had taken the boys to Missoula for a short summer vacation, Marissa was the only one at home.

There was nothing to distract her from thinking about the afternoon she'd spent with Brandon and his sweet kids. Jimmy and Maddie had tugged at her heartstrings, and for the first time, Brandon was opening up about being a single dad. But then she'd let her curiosity blow the day all to heck. Why in the world had she brought up the twins' mother? His response had sent her into a blue funk that was nearly impossible to kick.

She'd been able to handle the fact that he'd once cared about the woman. He'd stuck by her, even when she hadn't stuck by her own children. But when Brandon admitted that he hadn't wanted the felon the kids' mother loved to have any influence over Maddie and Jimmy, it felt as if her whole world, all her hopes and dreams, had suddenly fallen apart.

And while Marissa could certainly understand his concern, she'd realized that he might never fully trust her. Had he truly believed her explanation about her own incarceration?

When she'd asked about having the children spend the day with her at the ranch, for example, he hadn't jumped on the idea. And she wasn't going to bring it up again.

Monday was just as quiet and lonely, but she spent the day doing chores around the house and taking care of the garden—watering, weeding and picking the produce. She'd hoped Brandon would call her, but he hadn't. And she wasn't about to make the mistake of calling him.

There was no getting away from her past, she told herself as she stabbed a tool into a flower bed's soil. If Brandon couldn't deal with her unwarranted time in jail, well, okay. She'd need to accept it and move on. But truth be told, she didn't want to.

On Tuesday, as usual, she spent the morning working at Darla's. As soon as she arrived at the doughnut shop, her boss removed her apron. "I'm glad you're here. I have plenty of doughnuts, pastries and sweets made to last the morning, so I hope you don't mind if I cut out early. I have a migraine coming on. I need to go home, take some medication and try to sleep it off."

"No problem." Marissa had never been prone to headaches, but she'd heard migraines could be brutal. "I'll cover for you. And I'll lock up at two."

The morning began as usual, until a FedEx truck pulled up in front. The driver delivered an overnight delivery, a legal-size envelope addressed to Fred Garrison, Darla's husband. Marissa signed for it, then called Darla's house.

Fred answered on the second ring, the television blaring in the background. "Hello? Marissa? Hang on just a minute while I turn down the TV."

When the volume lowered, he asked if something was wrong.

"No," Marissa said. "Everything is fine here at the shop. But FedEx just delivered a large envelope for you. It looks important."

"You don't say." Fred cleared his throat. "I wasn't expecting that paperwork until later this week. But I'm glad it's there."

"I'd be happy to bring it to you after I lock up for the day," Marissa said. "Unless it can't wait. I can lock up the shop temporarily. Otherwise, I'll drop it off around two fifteen."

"It can wait until then. And thanks for bringing it to me. I'd really appreciate that. I'm supposed to stay off my foot, and Darla's taking a nap."

"Can she sleep through the telephone and television noise?"

"Yep. She's upstairs and all the way down the hall."

Good to know. "All right, then. I'll see you this afternoon."

As planned, Marissa locked up the doughnut shop a couple of minutes after two. Then, since she was still borrowing the ranch pickup until tomorrow, she drove the short distance to the Garrisons' house, which was located in a fairly new development, just off Oak Tree Drive.

She pulled along the curb, parked in front of Darla and Fred's two-story home and carried the package to the front door. Instead of ringing the bell, she knocked lightly.

"Come on in," Fred hollered.

Marissa opened the door and stepped into the spacious living room, where Fred sat in a brown leather recliner, his feet elevated. She crossed the room and handed him the envelope. "Here you go, Fred."

He thanked her, then proceeded to open it.

Marissa scanned the living room, noting the TV tray that sat next to Fred, the empty water glass, the dirty plate that must have held his lunch. "Can I get you anything while I'm here? A fresh glass of water?"

He looked up from his reading. "That'd sure be nice. Thank you."

She nodded, then scooped up the dishes and carried them to the kitchen, which was more than a little untidy. She prepared a glass of ice water, then after delivering it to Fred, she returned to clean up the mess neither Fred nor Darla should worry about today. She loaded the dishwasher, then filled the sink with hot soapy water and washed the pots and pans.

After she tidied up the kitchen, she used the soapy water in the sink to wipe down the counters. When she was satisfied with her work, she noticed a glass vase next to the stovetop.

A wistful smile crossed her lips. Her dad used to have one like that. A cut-glass Waterford vase that had been a wedding present. She wondered what had become of it. Suzanne had probably kept it without considering Marissa might want it to remember her parents by.

Oh, well. There wasn't anything she could do about that. But nevertheless, Darla's vase deserved to shine. The bouquet of flowers it once held had left a green, grungy film on the inside. So she carried it to the sink. As she lowered it into the water, it slipped from her grasp. She tried to catch it as it dropped, but it hit the edge of the sink and broke upon impact.

"Shoot!"

When she fished the broken pieces from the water, she cut her hand and pain seared through her. "Ow! Dang it."

She snatched her hand from the sink, but not before realizing the cut was deep. The water was tinged pink. She reached for a wad of paper towels and held them to the wound, but it bled through immediately. "Oh, man." She applied pressure over the one-inch gash to the side of her right hand, hoping that would help.

It didn't take a paramedic or a triage nurse to tell her she needed stitches. And that she'd have to drive herself to the clinic.

What luck. And now she'd need to tap into her savings to pay a medical bill. She'd also have to replace the vase. Could this week get any worse?

After settling a public disturbance at Town Square Park, which turned out to be an angry mother of a teenage boy challenging a bigger boy who'd been bullying him, Brandon headed toward his squad car, which he'd parked along the curb near the ball fields.

He was about to climb behind the wheel when he glanced across the street and spotted a familiar old pickup in one of the last parking spaces in front of the two-story redbrick medical building. Any of the Fairborn locals would recognize Jack McGee's old truck anywhere. If Alana was in Hawaii with her new husband, there was only one other person who might be driving it. His assumption proved true when he spotted Marissa heading toward the pickup, a purse slung over her shoulder.

They hadn't talked since the picnic on Sunday, and while he'd been a little hesitant in calling her afterward, he couldn't very well ignore her now. Neither did he want to. Instead of climbing into his squad car, he crossed the street and approached her.

"Hey," he called out.

She looked up and froze in mid-step. When their eyes met, she wore a suspect-in-the-headlights expression. He'd seen others do the same thing when they spotted him in uniform, most of them guilty about something. Odd, he thought. Then again, it probably had more to do with the conversation they'd had on Sunday afternoon.

His gaze lowered, and he noticed that she was holding a gauze-covered hand protectively against her chest. She'd apparently been hurt and must have come out of one of the medical offices.

His brow furrowed. "What happened?"

Her expression softened. She removed her injured hand from her chest. While holding it upright, she turned it slightly and looked at it. "This? Cut it on broken glass. It's not serious, but it needed a few stitches."

"Are you able to drive?" he asked.

"It's not a stick shift, so I can manage." She offered him a weak smile, yet her stance remained a little stiff. A little cool. Apparently, whatever had unsettled her on Sunday still bothered her.

"Is everything okay?" he asked.

"Sure." She offered up a smile. A really fake one.

Something was definitely off. Or rather, it was still off. She'd been pretty quiet on the ride home from the picnic, although she'd responded to the kids. Yet whatever had been wrong a couple of days ago seemed worse now, and he couldn't help thinking he was to blame.

Dammit. He should have called. It's not like he hadn't thought about her constantly.

Should he let her go? The radio he wore clipped to his belt squawked, signaling an incoming police call.

"You're busy," she said. "I'll see you around."

"We'll talk later, okay?"

"You bet." She didn't look at him, though. She just dug into her purse and pulled out the keys with her good hand.

He let her go. For now, anyway. Hell, he didn't have another choice. But tonight, after he got off duty, picked up the kids from preschool and asked Mrs. Hendrix to feed them dinner, he'd go to Rancho Esperanza and talk to her.

He answered the call and half listened as he watched her walk away, her steps quick. She unlocked the pickup and climbed inside.

It was time to have the chat with Marissa that he should have had before now.

Betty Sue had been seated in front of her favorite slot machine when Ralph came in and surprised the hell out of everyone at the market.

"Come on, honey. It's time. Please don't argue with me." Ralph slipped his arms around his wife and nuzzled her neck. "Let's trade in that minivan you've been driving and buy a new car for you."

Betty Sue damn near fell off her stool. "Well, run me over with an Oscar Mayer Wienermobile."

"Honey," Carlene said, "I really appreciate your suggestion. But I have two kids to haul around."

"You don't need a school bus to do that," Ralph said.

"Can I help you pick it out?" Betty Sue asked. "Carlene needs something red and sporty. Like a Porsche or a Corvette."

"Absolutely not," Carlene said. "But maybe something safe with a big back seat."

Yee-haw! Betty reached for her purse. "I'll go with you."

"Actually," Ralph said, "I'd rather you stayed here with Ella. I want to take Carlene to a late lunch."

Fair enough, Betty thought, although she didn't need a caretaker. If it was anyone other than Ella, she might have raised a stink. But she and the young woman had a connection.

So off the two lovebirds went. Betty Sue returned to her slot machine, and Ella straightened the shelves and rang up what few customers came in.

About forty-five minutes later, Ella said, "I'm going to the stockroom, Betty Sue. Will you watch the register for me?"

"You bet I will, sweetie." That's what Betty Sue liked about Ella. She didn't treat her with kid gloves, didn't treat her as if she was old and unable to look out for herself.

Betty Sue slid off her stool and made her way to the front counter. She'd no more than reached the register when a red pickup drove up. It had gun racks in back, which wasn't at all unusual around here. But when she spotted the driver, a big bulky guy wearing a sleeveless shirt, a chill wriggled down her spine. Apparently, his phone rang, and when he took a moment to answer it, Betty Sue snapped a picture of the guy with her cell, then she opened the register and removed a handful of cash and Ralph's extra set of keys. Then she hurried as fast as her arthritic knees would allow, ignoring the pain, and made it to the stockroom seconds later, huffing and puffing like an antique steam engine.

Ella looked up, the start of a smile forming on her face until she spotted Betty Sue. "What's wrong?"

"I think your jerk of a husband is out front." She showed the girl the picture.

Ella's face, as fair as she was, drained of color. "Oh, my god. He found me."

"That's what I thought." Betty Sue shoved Ralph's key fob into Ella's hand. "Get your purse, go into the bathroom and climb out the window. Take that truck and drive to the airport. Then use the cash to buy a ticket on the first flight out of Kalispell you can find. You're always welcome to come back when you feel safe."

Ella's whole body, as slender and frail as it was, shook so hard she could hardly grip the black fob. She started to move to the restroom, then hesitated. "I don't want to leave you here with him."

Betty Sue waved her off. "Get out of here. Stick Ralph's keys under the floor mat, and call me when you get someplace safe. I'll take care of things here."

Ella didn't argue. She took her bag from the shelf and slung it across her body. Then she stuffed the cash inside.

"Now, get a move on," Betty Sue said. "Circle around back and take the north road."

Ella hurried to the restroom with Betty Sue hobbling to keep up with her and watching as she tried to open the window. "Go. And be careful."

"It won't open."

The window was stuck. As Ella desperately tried to force it open, the glass broke. A shard nicked her hand as it fell to the floor. "Ow!"

"Dammit. Told you to be careful." Betty Sue took off her headscarf and wrapped it around Ella's palm. "I'll clean up. Get that dang window open and skedaddle."

Ella fought with the window frame until it finally gave way, providing an escape route. As she scurried out, Betty Sue closed the bathroom door and hobbled back to the front of the store, where the big ol' brute stood at the counter. "Hello, sir. How can I help you?"

"I'm looking for a woman."

"Sorry. Don't let the slot machine fool you. This isn't that kind of place."

"I'm not looking for *that* kind of woman." He handed over a photograph of Ella, blond hair hanging loose and free. "Have you seen *this* one?"

"Hmmm." Betty Sue pretended to study it long and hard. Ella had made some changes to her hair color and had cut it, but someone might still recognize the resemblance. "I think…maybe I did. A little gal who looked a lot like this stopped in a couple weeks ago. She asked for directions to Canada. Said she got a job and was relocating."

Ella's abuser glanced at the open register. In Betty's haste to grab the hundreds and fifties from under the till, she'd left the damned thing open. Plenty of fives, tens and twenties were still there, free for the taking.

Did the big brute plan to rob the market? Just in case, Betty reached for the gun Ralph kept behind the counter. Before she could raise it to scare him off, he grabbed it from her and gave her a shove. She lost her balance and fell. Her head struck the cigarette case hard and… She saw a glitter of stars until the lights went out completely.

Chapter Eleven

Brandon didn't get flustered during a crime report and investigation, but this was different. This
was his aunt and uncle and the only real family
he had.

When Dispatch had called him and reported
Tip Top Market had been robbed and that one
of the clerks, a female, had been assaulted and
was unconscious, his heart nearly dropped to the
pavement, and he couldn't get into his squad car
fast enough.

Brandon arrived at the market just as the am-
bulance was pulling out. When he saw his aunt
and uncle standing in the yard watching the para-

medics pull away, lights flashing, siren roaring, he was relieved. Thank God the injured clerk wasn't Carlene. It must be the new woman they'd hired.

He felt badly that their new employee had been injured. Maybe her job application would reveal her next of kin, someone who would be worried about her.

Carlene was in tears, and she slumped into Ralph's embrace. Money and stolen property could be replaced. He was glad the couple was safe. And that they had each other to lean on at a time like this.

As Brandon got out of the squad car, Ralph, his lip quivering, said, "I'm glad you're the one on duty today. When I asked the 9-1-1 operator who would be coming, she wouldn't say."

"What happened?"

"We left Ella, our new employee, in charge of the store and Betty Sue," Ralph said. "Then we came home to find Betty Sue bleeding and unconscious. Ella's gone. And so is my new truck. There's money missing from the register."

Ella? The woman his aunt and uncle insisted was working out well? That she tried hard, that she was good to Aunt Betty Sue?

He'd had a weird vibe about Ella when he learned Marissa and Alana had let a virtual stranger move in with them. "Did you talk to the references she listed on her job application? Did they give you any reason to be leery about hiring her?"

"I… Well, we didn't call anyone. Marissa vouched for her, and that seemed good enough for us."

"You should have called me," Brandon said.

"We didn't want to bother you. You've got the kids, a house, a job."

But background checks were a big part of his job.

"I never imagined this could happen," Carlene said. "Ella seemed to be responsible."

She certainly *did* seem responsible.

"All the large bills were stolen," Ralph said, "as well as some of the small ones. She took my keys, too."

"Who? Ella?" Brandon's brow furrowed.

Carlene clicked her tongue. "We aren't sure who did this. I just can't believe it was Ella. She wouldn't hurt Betty Sue. The two of them have gotten very close. In fact, Ella even comes to visit Betty Sue at the house. I know that there's a fifty-year age difference between them, but they like to go for walks together or hang out in Betty Sue's bedroom and chat and laugh."

Ralph huffed. "Maybe Ella was planning this all along, and Betty Sue got in the way. You just never know about people."

"No," Carlene said. "It wasn't her. Those two are kind of like a couple of teenage friends."

"*Friends* don't do things like this, honey."

Brandon agreed, but he kept his thoughts to himself.

Ralph placed a kiss on Carlene's brow. "I love you to pieces, but you've always been a little too trusting."

Brandon scanned the parking lot. The only vehicle there was a red Lexus SUV, the registration still taped to the windshield. "Whose car is that?"

"Your aunt's," Ralph said. "I just bought it for her today. That's where we were when this happened. At the dealership in Kalispell. Then we had lunch at a little French café she likes. When we got back here, we found Betty Sue unconscious and bleeding. Damn."

Right now, the perp was looking at charges of robbery, felony assault and grand theft auto. And, if Betty Sue died—God forbid—there'd be a felony murder charge. And like it or not, Ella, Betty Sue's new BFF, was a suspect. That is, unless the culprit had taken Ella with him against her will.

Brandon called Dispatch and asked them to send the crime-scene investigator out, then he told his aunt and uncle to wait in the parking lot while he entered the market.

Inside, he spotted the register, the till wide open. A few bills had been scattered on the floor.

Broken glass from the cigarette cabinet glistened in the overhead light. His stomach twisted. A puddle of Betty Sue's blood covered the floor.

Ralph's gun lay next to where Betty Sue had landed. Why hadn't the perp taken it? Had Betty Sue tried to use it in an attempt to defend herself?

Brandon made his way through the market, walking up and down the aisles. Nothing seemed to be out of place. He then entered the stockroom, which looked okay. The playroom his aunt and uncle had created for the kids appeared tidy.

He opened the bathroom door. The window was busted open. Most of the glass was outside, which meant whoever broke it was in the bathroom at the time. Why'd the perp exit that way? To avoid any possible surveillance cameras?

Too bad there weren't any. Brandon had wanted Ralph to put in a system, but he'd refused, saying they didn't need one, that folks around here were trustworthy.

It was also possible that a customer had driven up during the robbery and the perp or kidnapper wanted to escape unnoticed. Then again, why hadn't that customer called 9-1-1?

He stepped closer to the window and spotted blood on the glass, which meant the crime-scene investigator would swab it for DNA, as well as dusting for fingerprints.

He returned to the parking lot, where he found

his aunt and uncle. Ralph had just ended a phone call. His face was white, and his hands shook. "That was the ER doctor. Aunt Betty Sue suffered a very serious injury. They're still running tests, but they'll be putting her into a drug-induced coma to allow her brain to heal."

Carlene covered her mouth and choked back a sob. "I need to be at the hospital. I want to be there when she wakes up."

At her age, a fall and an injury like that could be life-altering, if not fatal.

"What do you know about your new employee?" he asked.

"Her name is Ella Perry," Ralph said. "She's twenty-seven. I'll get her job application for you. I can't remember where she came from, but she lives at Rancho Esperanza now."

He'd planned to stop by the ranch after work today so he could talk to Marissa. But he'd be heading over there now—on an official visit.

Before arriving at Rancho Esperanza, Brandon had gone over the job application Ella had filled out. But when he tried to verify her previous address and other significant details, he came up empty-handed. Ella Perry, if that was her real name, had lied. And sadly, his aunt and uncle had failed to call any of her references, which was too bad because she'd made them all up—names, addresses and phone numbers.

He'd been tempted to scold them for both being too trusting, for not being more careful, but a lot of good that would do after the fact. Besides, he should have been more involved in their hiring practices. He would have, if he hadn't cut back on their childcare hours. He'd thought he'd been doing them a favor.

Damn. Who asked for references, then failed to follow through on contacting them?

Either way, he was at Rancho Esperanza now. He knocked at the door, and moments later Marissa answered. Her pretty eyes widened at the sight of him, and while he felt an initial compulsion to offer her a friendly smile, this visit wasn't likely to be very friendly.

"I'm looking for Ella Perry," he said.

Marissa stiffened. "Is she in some kind of trouble?"

"I'm not sure. She's a person of interest in a robbery and an assault."

"Ella wouldn't do that," Marissa said.

"How do you know?"

"I just do. She's sweet and gentle to the point of almost being timid. If I'd had even the slightest concern about her honesty, I wouldn't have taken her to meet your aunt and uncle."

Was Marissa somehow involved? He hated to

think that, but he had to put his personal feelings aside and do his job.

He thought about the background check Greg had his P.I. friend run on her.

I hate to have to tell you this, Greg had said, *but Marissa Garcia has a record... Drug charge. Transporting. A year in county jail. After her probation was up, she moved away from San Diego. She's lived in Bakersfield, as well as Reno and Boise, and eventually landed in Fairborn.*

The same questions Brandon had that night came to mind. Why had she made so many moves? Why hadn't she stayed in one place very long?

Marissa opened the screen door and walked out onto the porch. Was there a reason she hadn't invited him in? One that had nothing to do with the chill he'd sensed when they'd gone to the park with the kids?

He glanced at her bandaged hand. Earlier today, before the call came in, he'd asked her what had happened.

Cut it on broken glass. It's not serious, but it needed a few stitches.

But what kind of glass? Had it been a broken window?

Could she be involved in the robbery at the market? With Ella?

No, that wasn't possible. Was it?

"Where were you this afternoon?" he asked. "Before you cut your hand?"

She paled, the color draining from her face, and her lips parted. "What are you suggesting, Brandon?"

"Someone robbed the market today."

Her jaw dropped. "And you think *I* was involved?"

"I'm just doing my job, Marissa. I'm investigating a robbery and an assault."

She swallowed, and her brow furrowed. "Who was assaulted?"

"Betty Sue. Someone knocked her unconscious, robbed the till and took off in my uncle's new truck."

"Oh, no! Not Betty Sue." Sympathy for the elderly woman soon gave way to the realization of what he'd implied. "And you actually think *I* had something to do with her getting hurt?"

"All I know is that Ella is missing. She's your friend, and you helped her get the job at the market. And there was a broken, blood-smeared window that was all in one piece when Ralph and Carlene left Ella in charge."

Marissa lifted her injured hand and shook it at him. "I worked at Darla's this morning. And when I locked up the shop, I delivered some paperwork to her husband, Fred. While I was there, I tidied up the kitchen and broke a crystal vase. So I have a valid alibi, Officer. Darla had gone to bed with a migraine and was asleep, but Fred Garrison can vouch for my whereabouts earlier today. He can also tell you how and where I cut my hand."

"All right," he said. "I'll talk to him. While I'm here, would you mind stepping aside and letting me take a look in Ella's room?"

She stiffened and folded her arms across her chest, taking care not to bump her bad hand. "Where's your warrant?"

"You don't have to get so defensive. I'm just doing my job. And looking out for my family."

"I got that. Loud and clear. So unless you have any other questions, Officer Dodd, I'm going to go back inside the house."

If she was as innocent as she claimed, he wouldn't blame her for being mad. But he still had to check out her alibi to be sure. He didn't mean to upset her, but he couldn't give her a free pass until his job was done.

Marissa felt like slamming the door in Brandon's face, but she kept her cool. Once it clicked shut and she turned the dead bolt, tears filled her eyes and streamed down her face.

He'd actually thought she might be involved in a robbery and an assault. But then again, why wouldn't he question her now? He'd run a background check on her already. Once a criminal, always a criminal, right?

She leaned her back against the door and slid down to the floor.

The cold, hard truth hit her like an avalanche, crushing her, making it hard to breathe. Brandon hadn't believed her when she'd told him she hadn't committed a crime. Clearly, he was never going to trust or believe her. And worse, anytime a crime happened in Fairborn, Marissa would be his first suspect. Always.

She'd paid her debt to society, one she'd never owed. Yet that didn't matter to Brandon.

And to think she'd actually flirted with the idea of dating him, of falling in love with him.

The ache in her heart tightened into a knot. Who was she kidding? She'd been dangerously close to falling in love with him, and even now, she couldn't ignore that fact. She shook her head. No, she was in love with him already. Dang it.

But Brandon had just burst her dream as if he'd poked a needle into a bright red balloon.

Marissa stood and wiped her face with her sleeves. She and Brandon were over. So she just had to put it behind her like every other unfair thing that had happened to her. But that wouldn't be easy. This betrayal, this pain was different. And she feared she would carry the heartache for a long, long time.

And what was more, Ella was missing. Betty Sue was gravely injured. And in her heart of hearts, Marissa knew Ella would never injure her friend.

It might be dinnertime, but she'd just lost her appetite.

A glass of wine sounded good. Not that she'd drown her sorrows. As she headed for the kitchen, her cell phone rang. She snatched it off the counter, not even bothering to look at the display. She assumed it was Brandon and answered without saying hello. "There's nothing to talk about."

"Yes, there is," Erik said. "Please don't hang up, Marissa."

Her blasted stepbrother. What was he doing calling her? Her fingers trembled, and she nearly dropped the phone. Erik had always been a charmer with a wild side. He'd been so good at snowballing their parents, and they'd never suspected a thing. Still, she'd actually looked up to the guy back then. That is, before he let her take the heat for a crime he'd committed.

"What do you want, Erik? I should just hang up on you."

"Please don't. I know you hate me, and I don't blame you. It was so wrong, so very wrong, for me to let you take the heat for the pills and the pot in the trunk. I had a serious drug problem back then, but last year, I joined Narcotics Anonymous."

Good for you, jerk. You didn't just ruin a year of my life, you've screwed up my future, too.

"I'm following the 12-Step Program. And I'd like to make amends with the people I've hurt— you being the one I hurt the most."

Great. Now he was using her to feel better about what he'd done. As if *I'm sorry* would erase all she'd gone through and the harm he'd caused.

"You're forgiven," she snapped. Now maybe he'd leave her alone. If he didn't, she'd change her number.

"Thanks. I know you'll need time to process this, and you may never truly forgive me. Maybe we can talk more about it at another time. But don't hang up. That's not the only reason I called."

Did Suzanne or his father die? Did he want to invite her to the funeral? Ha! Fat chance of that. She wouldn't attend, even if they lived across town, rather than fifteen hundred miles away.

Erik continued. "Did you know your father had set up an irrevocable life-insurance trust for you before he died?"

Her brow furrowed, and she clutched the cell tight. "What are you talking about?"

"Your dad's attorney called Suzanne. Once you turned twenty-five, the money was to be divided between the two of you."

"I had no idea." With the phone still pressed

against her ear, she walked to the sofa and plopped down.

"The lawyer said your father was well aware of the fact that you and Suzanne didn't get along very well."

"To say the least."

"Apparently," Erik said, "the trust was created out of your father's life-insurance policy. Your share is one hundred thousand dollars. But the money can't be divided until you both contact the bank in San Diego."

"Is this a joke? Another one of your schemes?"

"No, it's real." He paused. "I'm not like that anymore. I'm not."

She didn't respond. She wanted to believe him, but she couldn't make the leap.

After a few seconds of silence, he said, "Marissa? You still there?"

"Yeah, I need to wrap my head around this," Marissa said. "Can I give you a call tomorrow?"

"Sure. Anytime. I'll forward the info to you. What's your email address?"

She gave it to him, then he added, "Like I said, I'm really sorry."

"I heard you." It was the best response she could come up with since forgiveness wouldn't come easily.

She ended the call, trying to grasp all that Erik had told her, not just his admission of guilt and his apology. Had her father left her an unexpected gift?

Erik might be blowing smoke, but he'd seemed sincere. And the news finally began to sink in. One hundred thousand dollars.

If what he'd just told her was true, and that was still a big *if*, she'd have the money to pursue her dream of becoming a wedding planner. White Lace and Promises would soon become a reality, which was timely since she'd be able to build on the momentum from Alana and Clay's lovely wedding.

But the memory of Brandon standing on her porch in his sheriff uniform—and of his accusing gaze—washed over her. And she couldn't seem to muster any enthusiasm. Thanks to Brandon and his distrust of her, she couldn't join the Fairborn Chamber of Commerce because in a small town, the gossip would always be there. *Oh, Marissa Garcia? The woman Brandon dumped when he learned she'd spent time in jail? A criminal, no doubt.*

How could she possibly continue to live in Fairborn? This was Brandon's turf. And even if she could make a go of her business, even if she achieved success and community acceptance, she'd always be a criminal in the local deputy's eyes.

Marissa let out a groan and rubbed her eyes. Whine time. And time for a glass of wine.

She'd barely walked into the kitchen when her focus shifted from herself and anger at Brandon and Erik to concern for Ella.

The poor, battered woman. Was she safe?

Deep in Marissa's heart, she knew Ella wouldn't hurt Betty Sue. And she wasn't a thief. There had to be another explanation. Had someone else robbed the store and taken Ella hostage? That was possible, and Brandon had lost valuable time by not looking for her.

Then again, Doug Perry, Ella's abusive husband, might have found her. And if so, she was afraid he'd kill her, just as he swore he'd do if she ever left him again. Had she run away from him in desperation?

Marissa should have mentioned Ella's abuse to Brandon. Maybe she should call him now.

But what would she tell him? That Ella might be in jeopardy? That she wanted to file a missing-person report?

Yet that wouldn't explain the fact that Betty Sue had been severely injured. And that there'd been a robbery.

Her cell phone rang, drawing her from her thoughts. This time, she checked the display before answering.

"Thank God," Marissa uttered when she saw Ella's name. She didn't bother to say hello. "Where are you?"

"I'm in Seattle. I guess Betty Sue told you what happened. I was supposed to call her when I was safe, but her phone keeps rolling over to voice mail."

"Betty Sue is in the hospital. That's why she isn't answering."

Ella gasped. "Oh, no! What happened?"

"What do you mean *what happened*? I was going to ask you. You were there."

"She was fine when I left. Is she going to be okay?"

"I hope so. It's a head injury. I think it's pretty serious." Marissa let out a weary sigh. "What happened at the market today?"

Ella revealed the details, telling Marissa about Doug's arrival at the market, about Betty Sue warning her and insisting that she take Ralph's truck.

"I was so scared he would kill me. I would have frozen in fear, but Betty Sue took charge and told me what to do. Can you please let Ralph know that I left the pickup in the parking lot at the airport in Kalispell? Stall fifty-five. The keys are under the floor mat."

"Yes, of course. I'll tell him." Marissa combed the fingers of her good hand through her hair. "Brandon is investigating the incident as a robbery and an assault."

"Doug may be a brute, and he might have hurt

Betty Sue, but he's not a thief. At least, I don't think so."

"You have to call Brandon and explain what happened."

"I can't. My phone is about to die, and I don't have a charger. I'll have to buy one."

"Okay. But can you describe Doug? Do you know where he might have gone?"

Marissa took notes while Ella provided Doug's full name, date of birth and address. "I'll text you pictures of him standing beside his pickup truck. Hopefully, the license plate will be visible. You can also check Betty Sue's cell phone. She took a picture of him while he was outside the market."

"I'll handle it. Did you get a hotel room?"

No answer. "Ella?"

Ella's phone was dead. But thank God *she* was alive. That was the best news Marissa had heard all day. She now had the information Brandon needed to find the real culprit and to clear Ella's name. And hers, too.

But it wouldn't repair Marissa's relationship with Brandon. Or allow her to remain in Fairborn any longer. At this point, she needed another fresh start.

Chapter Twelve

Brandon had just put the twins to bed when he got a call from Marissa. He had no idea what she had on her mind, although he hoped she'd tell him she was sorry she'd gotten angry at him and that she understood he was just investigating a crime in which the victims had been his family members.

Okay. Maybe he hadn't handled the interview very well. But getting the facts sometimes meant being tough.

"Hey," he said. "What's up?"

"I heard from Ella. She left your uncle's pickup

in the parking lot at the airport in Kalispell. The keys are under the mat."

Brandon hadn't seen that coming. "Ralph will be happy to hear that."

"She also told me what went down at the market today, although I doubt you'll take my word for it."

He probably ought to apologize, but he wasn't sorry for doing his job. "Why don't you start by telling me her version of the story." Of course, at this point, Ella's version was the only one he had to go on.

"I'll start by telling you that Ella is a victim of domestic violence. Her husband used to beat the crap out of her, and a couple of weeks ago, she finally ran away from him. But he came looking for her. Focus your investigation on Douglas Raymond Perry, who lives in Coeur d'Alene, Idaho. And if you don't want to take Ella's word for it, check Betty Sue's cell phone. Your aunt took a picture of him while he was standing outside the market. And once Ella is able to recharge her cell phone, she's going to send me some pictures of him. When she does, I'll forward them to you."

"Are you saying Ella's husband is responsible for the robbery?"

"I don't know about that. There might not have been a robbery. Ella said Betty Sue gave her the cash to escape, along with your uncle's keys. I have no idea what happened after that, but my guess is that Betty Sue and Doug Perry had a run-in at the cash register."

"I'll get right on it."

A cool silence filled the line until Marissa asked, "How's Betty Sue? Is she doing any better?"

"No. I talked to Ralph earlier. She's still in a medically induced coma, but the doctor mentioned that they may bring her out of it in a couple of days."

"I'm praying for her."

"Thank you. We appreciate that." He paused for a moment, trying to gather his thoughts, to say the right thing in the right way. Then he blew out a sigh. "I'm sorry if I hurt your feelings. It wasn't personal."

She waited a beat, then said, "It was personal for me. Apparently, you don't know me as well as you think you do."

Maybe not, but from what he'd learned so far, she'd been honest with him all along. And he hadn't trusted her.

"Like I said, I was just doing my job."

"Today, maybe. But running a background check on a woman you wanted to date? I think that's a little over the top. Maybe that's common procedure for cops, but it doesn't work for me."

It had been Greg's idea. But Brandon wasn't

going to blame anyone other than himself. He'd given Greg the okay. And any other excuse he might have had at the time escaped him now. "I'm sorry, Marissa. I was wrong."

"Yes, you were. Someday you're going to make a mistake, and when that happens, hopefully, whoever you've wronged will have a bigger heart than you have. And they'll be more willing to forgive."

"Can we start over?" he asked.

"We never got started," she said, her soft and weary tone tearing at his heart. "Good night, Brandon."

The line disconnected before he could respond.

The next morning, Marissa purchased an airline ticket and told Erik she was on her way. Even though she saw the flight to San Diego as a business trip and wasn't excited about sitting down in the same room with Suzanne, it was a good excuse to get out of town.

She packed light, since she wasn't going to stay any longer than necessary. After placing a second pair of jeans into her overnight bag, she reached into the closet to remove a white blouse. She'd just begun to fold it when her cell phone rang. A glance at the display told her it was Brandon. She was tempted to let it roll over to voice mail, but she answered it anyway, her tone revealing her pain and disappointment. Then she put it on speaker so she could finish packing.

"What's up?" she asked.

"Douglas Perry was arrested last night," Brandon said. "For assault and, depending upon what the crime-scene investigators learn about his intent, he could be charged with attempted murder."

"Good." At least Brandon had listened to her and followed through accordingly.

"Perry also had an outstanding warrant for his arrest. He was out on bail and wasn't supposed to leave the state."

"What was he arrested for?"

"A couple of weeks ago, after Ella left him, he went to a bar and downed more than his share of whiskey. On his way home, he was involved in an accident. It wasn't his first DUI, and he failed to show up for court-ordered rehab. So he'll be locked up for a while."

Thank goodness. "Ella will be relieved to hear that."

"Will you let her know that it's safe for her to return to Fairborn now?"

"Sure." Marissa placed a plastic bag filled with her makeup and toiletries into her carry-on. "How's Betty Sue? Is she doing any better?"

"She's not fully conscious yet, but she's responsive. So the doctors are optimistic."

"I'm glad to hear that." She zipped her bag shut. "I'd like to visit her when I get back."

"Where are you going?"

It really wasn't his business, but there was no reason to be rude or snarky. "San Diego."

"To see your family?"

"It's not a social visit, but I'll see them while I'm in town."

"How long will you be gone?" he asked.

It didn't really matter. Even when she returned to Fairborn, she wouldn't stay in town much longer. "A couple of days."

"When you get back, I'd like to take you to lunch. Or maybe meet you for coffee. We need to talk."

She blew out a weary sigh. "There's nothing to talk about. I've already told you how I feel. Besides, I won't have time. Katie Johnson, who lives here with her younger brothers, and I volunteered to watch the ranch and feed the stock while Alana is on her honeymoon. I'm not going to dump the full responsibility on Katie, but as soon as Alana and Clay return, I'm leaving town. I've already given notice to Darla and Tameka."

"Please don't go. That's not necessary. I was wrong, and I'm sorry. You've proven time and again that you're loyal. And you have a kind heart."

Marissa sucked in a deep breath, then slowly

blew it out. "I accept your apology, Brandon. But whatever we may have had or tiptoed around is over. You'll never really trust me. You'll always be a cop, and you'll never forget that I'm a convicted felon."

"That's not true."

"Oh, no? You wouldn't even let me be around your kids without a chaperone present." And the fact that he didn't trust her to be good to those two precious kids had crushed her.

He didn't respond right away, probably chewing on the truth. But she didn't have time to defend herself or to state her case.

"I need to go, Brandon. I have a plane to catch." Then she ended the call. And ended things with him once and for all.

Last night, after Brandon fed the kids dinner, supervised their baths and got them ready for bed, Marissa had remained on his mind. Even the bedtime story Jimmy and Maddie had chosen for him to read was about a cat named Marissa. Who in the hell would dub a cat with that name?

There's nothing to talk about.

I'm leaving town.

Whatever we had is over.

The thought of her leaving hit him like a rock to the solar plexus. And he'd slept like hell.

After dropping off the twins at preschool, he

called his uncle to ask if Betty Sue was doing any better.

"The nurse told me she had a good night," Ralph said. "She's conscious now. So Carlene is going to watch the market, and I'm going to the hospital. Visiting hours start at eleven."

"Want to meet me for a cup of coffee before then?" Brandon asked.

"Sure. I'll see you at The Jumping Bean in an hour."

An hour later, as Brandon and Ralph shared an outdoor table at Fairborn's newest coffee shop, Brandon tried to figure out a way to bring up the subject of Marissa and his feelings about her. But all he ended up doing was fussing with a paper napkin, rolling a corner up, then unrolling it.

"Something on your mind?" Ralph asked.

"Is it that obvious?"

"On you? Yes, it is." Ralph opened a sugar packet and poured it into his heat-resistant paper cup. "You've always been good at keeping your thoughts and feelings close to the vest. But you're perplexed about something."

Brandon blew out a sigh. "It's Marissa. We've been…sort of seeing each other. But I'm afraid I've really botched things up with her." He went on to explain what he'd done—the background check, the false assumption he'd made about her being involved in a robbery that never actually happened. And he didn't hold back.

"A relationship requires trust," Ralph said. "And sometimes that means choosing to trust, even when you have reason not to."

"I'm not sure I'm following you."

Ralph took a deep breath, then slowly let it out. "About twenty years ago, I had an affair."

Seriously? "I had no idea."

"No, why would you? I'm not proud of it. I can try to explain what I did and why, but I can't. It was a horrible mistake." Ralph sat back in his seat, his shoulders slumping at the guilty admission that he clearly hated to make.

"What caused you to do it?" Brandon asked.

"It happened during a time our marriage was a little shaky. Your aunt and I had been arguing a lot, and she said she needed some time away. A cooling-off period. So she went to visit a friend in Missoula. I went to Sully's Pub one evening, and I met a woman. She had a nice smile and was a good listener. She made me feel special. And one thing led to another." Ralph gave a little shrug. "It just happened."

"And Carlene found out?"

Ralph nodded. "One of the women in her bridge group spotted me with someone else and told her. I figured all hell was going to break loose when she found out. We'd had some loud arguments in the past, but not that time. Carlene was crushed, which only made me feel guiltier than ever."

"How did you earn her trust again?"

"She eventually forgave me, but the trust? It was shattered. I could have apologized until the birds flew south for the winter, but Carlene—God bless her—chose to trust me. And I gotta tell you, I've spent the last twenty years proving to her that she made the right decision."

Brandon took a sip of coffee, letting his uncle's confession seep in.

"Take it from me," Ralph added, "we all make mistakes, son. If you love Marissa, you'll have to go hat in hand and ask her to forgive you. And if she turns you away, try again. Because true love is worth fighting for."

"As long as I don't turn into a stalker."

Ralph laughed. "You won't. I suspect from the way she looks at you, she feels the same way."

"Maybe." Did he love her?

If he didn't, then why did it hurt so bad to lose her?

He'd have to convince her that he trusted her completely. He just wasn't quite sure how to go about it, especially since she had every reason to believe he'd betray her again.

Marissa's flight to San Diego arrived on time. After making her way through the airport with her carry-on, she waited at the curb until Erik picked her up. She had to admit, he looked a lot better than he had the last time she'd seen him—the day she'd been arrested and he'd clammed up and refused to take personal responsibility.

He'd been too thin, and his otherwise-tanned complexion looked as if he'd hibernated all winter in a bat cave. He was bulkier now. Healthier, it seemed. He appeared calmer, too. Before, he'd either been hyper or sullen and moody. Today he was neither.

They didn't talk much as he drove her downtown, where she was to meet Suzanne at the attorney's office. She wasn't looking forward to seeing her stepmother again, but she was ready to put this part of her life behind her.

She'd told Erik that she forgave him, but she still felt resentful. And doubtful. She'd never forget what he'd put her through and the blemish it had left on her reputation, the ugly mark it had left on her heart. He'd hidden his drug addiction from their family and left her to take the blame for his crime.

"We're here," he said, as he pulled into the driveway that led to an underground garage, and parked the older Toyota 4Runner. They didn't talk. After they entered the lobby, they took the elevator to the eighth floor.

When they reached the attorney's office, Marissa spotted Suzanne seated in a reception area and paused in the doorway. The tall blonde, her hair cut in a chic bob, stood and offered a weak smile. But Marissa couldn't seem to return it. Even a cool greeting would have been as fake as Suzanne's tan.

"It's nice to see you," Suzanne said. "I'm glad you're here."

Seriously? Was she actually glad to see Marissa? Or just eager to get her share of the trust?

"I bet you are," Marissa said, not looking at the woman. "Let's get this over with."

"I owe you an apology," Suzanne added. "I believed Erik when I shouldn't have. I don't blame you if you find it hard to forgive me. I'll never forgive myself." She reached into her purse, pulled out a business card and handed it to Marissa. "If you ever want to talk, you can reach me at my real-estate office."

Marissa glanced at the glossy card, and while she couldn't see any reason to ever contact her stepmother, she slipped it into the front pocket of her jeans. "Sure. Whatever."

Suzanne's lips pulled to the right, then to the left. "I'd like to take you to dinner tonight. I hope you'll agree. In the meantime, I'll leave you to talk to your father's attorney. I've already signed off on the paperwork. I want you to know, I'm not taking my share of the trust."

Marissa furrowed her brow. "Excuse me?"

"I'd like you to have it all. It won't make up for my lack of support during your trial and…and your incarceration, but I hope it will convince you of how very, very sorry I am."

Either this was some kind of scam or Marissa hadn't heard her right. She didn't know what to believe. Or what to say. *Thank you? I accept your apology? Dinner sounds great? What's in it for you?*

"You might find this hard to believe, Marissa. But I want nothing more than for you to forgive me. And I hope you'll call me. About dinner tonight."

Marissa gaped, didn't know how to respond. This turn of events had her mind wheeling.

"But whether you forgive me or not, I wish you the best." Suzanne offered another smile, this one stronger than the last. But was it sincere? Was it some kind of a trick?

She turned and walked out the door, her stilettos clicking down the hallway as she made her way to the elevator.

Erik touched her elbow. "She means it, Marissa. She's really sorry. And so am I. After everything that went down, I know we'll never be a real family again, but we can be civil."

Marissa stepped back. "I suppose. But I'm

not sure if I'll ever be able to trust either of you again."

"That's fair," Erik said.

A balding man in his fifties entered the reception area.

"Marissa Garcia?" he asked.

Words escaped her, but she nodded.

"I'm Grant Collins, your father's attorney and the trustee of the insurance trust. Come on back to my office. I have the documents ready for you to sign. My paralegal is also a notary, so once you have them in hand, you can go directly to the investment bank that holds the account. It's all yours. So you can either leave it invested or take the cash."

"All right." Marissa glanced at Erik, who took a seat next to the chair Suzanne had vacated.

"I'll wait here for you," he said. "Then I'll take you wherever you want to go."

Marissa had no idea where she wanted to go, or what she wanted to do. She had more options now than she'd ever had, and her mind was spinning. But in the meantime, she followed Mr. Collins to his office.

Betty Sue reached for the bedside remote and raised her head so she could get a better look at her new room. They'd moved her out of ICU earlier today, thank goodness. And if she was lucky, the doctor was going to release her to go home tomorrow.

Carlene, who was seated in the chair next to the bed, said, "I talked to Ella this morning. She told me how brave you were. She was able to escape thanks to your clear head. And then you went to face that horrible man by yourself. I'm proud of you."

"Oh, yeah?" Betty Sue chuckled. "I'm a tough old bird. So cut me some slack. And don't treat me like an invalid when I get home."

"I'll try to remember that." Her tone rang guilty, and she kept her focus on the speckled linoleum floor.

"Good." Betty Sue shrugged. "And I'll try not to wander without letting you know what I'm up to. Except when I go to the Grange Hall to play bingo. I've got my eye on Earl Hoffman, the bartender who works at most of the events held there. And I'd hate to have you mess things up for me."

Carlene raised her hand in Scout's-honor fashion. "I promise."

"Then, it's a deal." Betty Sue glanced at the doorway and spotted Marissa holding a flower arrangement and looking a little sheepish, like she wasn't sure if she should make her presence known or slip off and give them some privacy.

"Come on in," Betty Sue said. "Don't be shy, honey."

Marissa slowly made her way into the room. "I hope I'm not intruding."

"You aren't. We're just chatting. No big deal." Betty Sue reached for her glass of water and, using the straw, took a couple of sips. The white-board next to the television listed the date and the name of the nurse who was taking care of her today: Patricia M. "It's Thursday. Isn't that your day to work at the doughnut shop?"

"I took some time off," Marissa said. "I flew to San Diego for a night. I just got back and thought I'd stop by to see how you're doing."

"I'm a little banged up. But it's just a flesh wound. Seems like everyone thinks I nearly kicked the bucket, but I'm still here."

Marissa made her way to the tray table. "I brought you some roses. Would you like me to place them here? Or maybe near the sink, where you can see them?"

"Put them by the window." Betty Sue fingered the gauze bandage on her head, the badge of cour-age she'd received after her run-in with the brute who'd come looking for Ella. She would have shot him, but he got the jump on her. Twenty years ago—hell, five years ago—he wouldn't have stood a chance.

Someone rapped on the doorframe and cleared their throat. Betty Sue glanced up to see Bran-don wearing his uniform. He was a handsome man—and the kind a young woman could look up to even if she'd been pulled over for a traffic infraction.

"Looks like we're having a party. Come on in."

He stood in the doorway a moment. His gaze landed on Marissa's, and she stiffened.

Betty eyed them carefully. Hmm. Trouble in paradise, it seemed.

As Brandon made his way to Betty Sue's bedside, he offered her a grin. "How are you doing?"

"Not bad, although I'd feel a lot better if I was at home."

"I'm sure you would." Brandon returned his attention to pretty Marissa, whose skittish demeanor suggested she'd like an excuse to bolt.

Carlene got to her feet. "We're only supposed to have two visitors at a time, so—"

"I'll go," Marissa blurted out.

"No, you won't." Carlene started toward the door. "You just got here. I'll take off and come back this evening. Is there anything I can bring you, Betty Sue? Anything you need?"

A big ol' smirk stretched across Betty Sue's face. "How about a bottle of Jack Daniel's?"

"I'll bring a milkshake instead." Carlene chuckled as she walked out of the room.

"Extra whipped cream, then," Betty Sue called out.

They made idle chitchat for a couple of minutes, then Brandon said, "If you don't mind, I'd like to take Marissa outside. There's something I want to talk to her about."

"Feel free to have that little chat right here," Betty Sue said. "I'll ask the nurse to bring another chair."

"Thanks for the hospitality," Brandon said. "But I need to talk to her privately."

Marissa rolled her eyes.

Betty Sue figured the girl wasn't up to hearing whatever Brandon was about to say. She had no idea what Brandon had done, but from Marissa's huff, it was something he needed to apologize for.

"Go ahead, then." She waved them off. Then she crossed her fingers, hoping the boy made things right.

And that Marissa would forgive him.

Chapter Thirteen

Brandon hadn't expected to see Marissa at the hospital, but he was glad they'd run into each other. And he was relieved that she'd agreed to talk to him. He just wished he wasn't wearing his uniform. He knew that put her off.

As they left the room, their shoes tapping on the polished tile floor, he started to turn right and down the corridor, but Marissa stopped in her tracks. "Where are you going?"

"There's a memorial garden right off the lobby," Brandon said, expecting her to continue walking with him.

Marissa tucked a silky strand of hair behind her

ear, revealing the pretty topaz studs. "Whatever you have to say, you can say it here."

He stepped closer to her, and her alluring scent, something lightly floral and springtime fresh, filled the air, taunting him. Damn, she looked good today. She wasn't wearing anything fancy— just a white blouse and a pair of jeans that hugged her curves.

She eased away from him and said, "What is it you want to say?" A frown and her serious tone let him know how badly he'd hurt her.

"I…"

She folded her arms across her chest, protectively, blocking her heart. And shutting him out.

Okay. He got that. So he tried another tactic, a neutral one. "How was your trip to San Diego?"

Her stance softened. Slightly. "Better than I expected."

She looked away and nodded to a doctor passing by, a faint smile aimed at that guy.

She'd only been gone for a night, but he'd missed her something fierce. He'd never felt such a longing for a woman before, and it rocked him to his core. Had he lost her for good?

"I'm actually thinking about moving back home," she added.

He stiffened. "Home? As in San Diego?" He didn't want her moving anywhere, especially more than a thousand miles away. "I thought you left to get away from your family."

"I did. But they're trying to make amends."

"After all they did, all they didn't do, you can forgive them?"

"I've thought about it a lot. I should try. They gave me reason to believe they were truly sorry."

A glimmer of hope raced through him. Could he give her reason to believe *he* was truly sorry?

"So what did you want to talk to me about?" she asked, looking at her watch.

Okay, here goes. He sucked in a breath, then let it out slowly. "To tell you that I screwed up royally. I should have trusted you completely, and I promise to do that from now on. I hope you'll forgive me."

She glanced down at her feet and didn't respond. He didn't push. He let her have the time to think, to consider what he'd said. And, hopefully, time for her to soften even more.

She finally looked up and spoke. "Remember when I asked if I could take the kids to spend time with me on the ranch?"

He nodded.

"You didn't answer right away. And when you did, you said, 'Maybe. Someday.' I realized you weren't comfortable with me being alone with them, and that hurt."

He ran a hand through his hair. So that had

been the tipping point. At least he knew it now. Maybe he could explain in a way she'd understand. "Mostly, the question surprised me. And since my kids really like you, I didn't want them to feel badly if things didn't work out between us."

She clicked her tongue. "Be honest. You also didn't trust me."

True. And he couldn't argue. "I know I tend to be skeptical of people. It's who I am—and a result of my childhood. But it also comes with the job."

"I sensed that. Thanks for confirming it." She looked at her watch again.

He was losing her, and a sense of panic set in. "No, wait. I think you misunderstood me. I know you're a good person—honest, loyal and loving. And I trust you. Completely. Will you give me a chance to prove it?"

She slowly shook her head. "I'm sorry, Brandon. I can't give you that chance. I have too much going on in my life right now."

"Like what? Maybe I can help you find a balance. What are you dealing with?"

"I need to decide where to open my business. I want to be a wedding planner. And a party planner."

"Fairborn would be the perfect place. I've got some money saved. I'd be happy to invest in your venture. Or loan you the money." Hell, he'd even give it to her. He was getting desperate to make things right between them.

"I like you, Brandon. I might even love you. But I don't need your help." She waited a beat. "Or you."

His heart pounded. "Come on, please. You're giving your family a second chance. How about giving me one, too?"

"I'm sorry," she said, unfolding her arms. "I can't do this right now."

"Why not?"

She looked at him with beautiful, soulful eyes that glistened with hurt. "Because you broke my heart."

And now she was breaking his.

As they gazed at each other, he fought the urge to hold her in his arms to comfort her, but he'd blown his chances with her.

"Listen," she said, shaking her head as though to rid her emotions. "I need time. And space. It's not just you, it's me." She nodded down the hall, toward the elevator. "I'm going back to the ranch. Tell Betty Sue I said goodbye. I'll see her again before I leave town."

Brandon grabbed her arm, his grip firm at first, then loosening. "You go visit her. I'll give you the time you need. But know that I'll always be there for you. If you'll have me." Then he released her and walked away.

His steps echoed down the hall as he made his way to the elevator. She'd said she might even love him. So he might still have a chance to convince her.

Only trouble was he had no idea where to go from here.

When Brandon walked into the hospital room wearing his uniform, all Marissa could see was his badge—and the man behind it, the guy who'd always be a cop, who'd always be on the lookout for a crime ready to happen, a criminal to apprehend.

She'd wanted nothing more than to take him at his word, to know that he was truly sorry, that things would be different between them from here on out. But she knew that wasn't to be.

She let out a sigh and paused before the doorway to Betty Sue's room. Closing her eyes, she rested her forehead against the doorframe.

When a frail, wrinkled arm reached out and grabbed her hand, she nearly jumped out of her skin. "Betty Sue! You scared the heck out of me. What are you doing out of bed?"

"Listening in on the conversation you were having with my nephew. And planning to chase after you if I had to. Come in here, girl. We need to talk." The elderly woman held her IV pole in one hand and pulled Marissa into her room with the other. The strength of her grip was surprising.

"You're not supposed to be walking around. You just got out of the ICU. Do I have to call the front desk?"

"Don't be a tattletale. I'm fine. Patricia, my nurse, is a tiny little thing. She won't put up much of a fight. Besides, I'm just trying to take care of my family. Now, come in and sit down. You and I are going to have a little chat."

When Marissa was seated and Betty Sue had scrambled back into bed, all the anger, the sorrow, the grief she'd choked down over the years bubbled to the surface, and she couldn't hold in the tears any longer. "I'm sorry." She sniffled. "This is so unlike me. I don't usually cry. And certainly not in front of anyone."

"Let it out, honey. I get the feeling you have a lot to cry about."

As if finally having an opportunity to let it all loose, the words rolled right out of her mouth, and she told the elderly woman everything—about her dad's unexpected death, her stepmother's resentment, Erik's betrayal and her efforts to find a place where she could put down roots and start fresh.

She had to take a moment to catch her breath, to avoid hyperventilating after her long, rambling spiel. "I finally landed in Fairborn."

"Go on," Betty Sue said. "Don't stop now."

Marissa blew out a ragged sigh. "I've made friends here. I like living at Rancho Esperanza. But then…"

"Along came Brandon."

Marissa nodded. "I didn't realize he was a deputy sheriff. I just thought he was a gorgeous guy and a wonderful father. I adore the twins." She paused, wondering if Betty Sue would understand. Or if she'd take Brandon's side. After all, they were family, and blood ran deep.

But something told her Betty Sue wasn't a typical relative. She cut a glance at the woman sitting upright in her hospital bed, and the words, the hurt tumbled out again. "Did you know that he had the gall to run a background check on me? I mean, who does that to a woman he wants to date?"

Betty Sue clucked her tongue. "You got me there. No wonder you're mad at him. But don't forget Brandon is a cop. He's trained to look beyond the obvious. He has that sort of mind and the investigation tools at his disposal."

"So you're telling me he doesn't trust anyone?"

Betty Sue shrugged. "I think it's more like *Trust but verify.* He has two sweet kids. He's going to protect the public, but believe me, he's going to protect his family first."

"You're right. And I could have forgiven him for that, but after the so-called robbery and the assault, he came to the ranch and practically accused me of being a coconspirator with Ella." She lifted her injured hand, which bore only a regular bandage now and not one made of gauze. "He wanted to run a DNA test to see if it was my blood on the broken window at the market. Can you believe that?"

"He was doing his job. He obviously cares for you, so it must have been hard on him, too, don't you think?"

"I guess." Was she being self-centered and not taking into consideration how Brandon felt? How he had a job to do?

Betty Sue clicked her tongue and slowly shook her head. "So what are you going to do about your situation?"

"Relocate. I might even go back to San Diego. I was there yesterday, and my family… Well, they seem to be really sorry for what went down. And they're trying to make it up to me."

"Are you kidding? After all they did to you? You're thinking about forgiving them?"

"Yeah. Is that crazy?"

Betty Sue looked Marissa up and down. "It's actually very healthy as long as you don't get sucked back into their drama. But how about Brandon? Are you going to give him a chance?"

"I don't know. I feel so scattered and so broken

inside, I don't know what to do. All I know is that I can't deal with his trust issues."

"Maybe you have those issues, too. Consider trusting that what he says is true. You seem to be doing that with your family. It's called taking a leap of faith."

She had a point, Marissa supposed. "I just don't know if I can jump that high."

"Listen," Betty Sue said, "I'm going to tell you about the great love of my life. Like Ella, I was a battered woman, too. And I was able to escape. But I built a wall around my heart, determined not to trust the wrong guy again."

"The love of your life hit you?"

"No. Not him. But I was leery of trusting anyone ever again. So I broke up with my Mr. Right before he could do me wrong."

"There's nothing wrong with trying to protect yourself."

"True." Betty Sue crossed her arms. "But there is if you shut out true love. Rumor had it that my old lover took it hard, that my leaving town really tore him up. And eventually, I returned, thinking I'd give him another chance. But it was too late. He was with another woman, and she was obviously pregnant. With his baby."

"Maybe I need to go away for a while."

"Oh, for Pete's sake. You're going to run away? Don't do that. You're at a crossroads. It's called fight or flight. If Brandon was a grizzly bear—or God forbid, a brute like the one who used to beat on Ella—I'd say run like hell. But Brandon's not like that. He's also teachable. So in this case, I'd suggest you fight."

"Fight for him?"

"Heck, no. Don't fight *for* him. There's no one standing in the way other than you and him. So fight *with* him. Tell him how you feel. Tell him that he'd better cut the skepticism crap when it comes to you. Stand up for yourself. Demand respect. Brandon doesn't get to make all the rules, right?"

Marissa gazed at the wise woman: something warm and maternal burned bright in her. An understanding, a kindness and support that had always been lacking in Marissa's life. She'd never known her mom, and she'd once hoped to see something similar in Suzanne's eyes.

She brushed at the tears that began to slide down her cheeks, and she choked back a sob to no avail.

Betty Sue opened her arms, offering a hug. "Come here, honey. Let it out."

Marissa accepted her comforting embrace, and the sweet, quirky old woman held her while she cried. When her sobs finally subsided, Betty Sue released her.

"Thanks so much for listening to me. And for

your advice. Has anyone ever told you that you'd make a good counselor?"

"No one in my family. But I've always known it." Something wistful clouded her eyes, then she smiled. "Maybe I should go back to school."

Marissa wouldn't put anything past the spunky woman. "You don't need a degree to help people, Betty Sue."

"I know. But I may as well get one. I only have one more class to take for a master's degree in psychology."

"Seriously?"

Betty Sue chuffed. "I hate science, and there was a graduate-level human biology course I was supposed to take. But with my social security and pension, I can afford a tutor these days."

"You're something else."

"So are you, honey. And don't you ever forget it."

Marissa certainly would remember this conversation for the rest of her life. She just wasn't sure where she'd be spending it. Or if she'd be spending it with Brandon.

Brandon needed to talk to someone, a guy his age, a friend he respected. So while he was on his way to the preschool to pick up the twins, he called Mrs. Hendrix and asked if Maddie and Jimmy could have dinner with her.

"That would be great. I hate eating alone, and I love to cook. I'll think of something kid-friendly to make, like fried chicken. Would they like that?"

"Don't bother cooking tonight. I'll pick up a pizza on our way home."

"Do you have to work late?" his kindhearted neighbor asked.

"Actually, I need to talk to a friend. A guy I went to high school with."

"That's nice. Men like you need some downtime."

That was true. And boy oh boy, did Brandon need some downtime. He'd always been able to think himself out of a dilemma. But the one he was facing with Marissa was a biggie. Ralph had suggested that he keep at it, that he not give up. And that's what Brandon thought he'd been doing. But it hadn't worked. In fact, he'd probably made things worse outside the hospital room.

Damn. He needed a second opinion.

When the twins got into the car, Jimmy said, "I smell pizza."

Both kids clapped and cheered.

"I'm taking you over to Mrs. Hendrix's house for dinner. And you're going to stay with her for a while."

"Why?" Maddie asked. "Are you going to work?"

"No, I'm going to see Greg."

"You guys having a playdate?" Jimmy asked.

"Yeah. Something like that."

An hour later, after calling Greg and delivering the twins and the pizza to Mrs. Hendrix, he'd gone to his house, showered and put on his favorite pair of jeans and slipped on a T-shirt. Then he drove to Sully's Pub, where he found his buddy waiting, a longneck bottle of Corona in hand.

"Damn." Greg stretched out his long legs and crossed his ankles while watching Brandon take a seat across from him. "You might have showered and gotten comfortable, but you look like hell. What happened?"

"I crashed and burned with Marissa." Brandon motioned for the cocktail waitress. When she stopped by the table, he nodded at Greg's longneck bottle. "I'll have a beer, too."

Once she left them alone, he launched into the problem he had with Marissa, the wall she'd backed him into.

Greg let out a slow whistle. "I feel for you, man. Shelley just cut me loose, too."

"I'm sorry."

Greg waved him off. "No big. I'll get over it."

Brandon sat back in his seat and studied his friend. "You seem to be taking it well."

"Yeah, well, she said it was just a physical thing for her. And when push came to shove, it was for me, too. It still stung—if you know what I mean. No one likes to be used."

Brandon nodded, thinking about his ex and the kids' mom.

"But what the hell. Another woman will come along."

For Greg, maybe. But Brandon didn't think another woman would do the trick for him.

"Man." Greg leaned forward and scrunched his brow. "You look like someone kicked you to the curb."

Brandon blew out a sigh, then told his friend the entire saga, how Marissa had pushed him away at the hospital. "She gave me the standard woman's breakup lines—all of them. 'I need time. And space. It's not you, it's me.'"

"Ouch. So, it's over?"

"Yeah. Probably."

The cocktail waitress brought his beer, and he thanked her. Then he took a big, thirst-quenching, guilt-easing sip. But even that didn't help.

"Probably?" Greg sipped his beer. "There's hope somewhere in that story?"

"She said she thought she was in love with me."

Greg pointed his longneck bottle at Brandon. "Then, you have a chance."

Brandon looked up. "You think?"

"All you have do is prove to her that you trust her."

"How?" Brandon rolled his eyes. "I've told her a hundred times. She won't listen."

"I said *prove* it. Show her."

"How in the hell am I supposed to do that?"

Greg shrugged. "Wish I could tell you, bro. You know her better than I do."

Then an idea came to him. One that just might work.

Chapter Fourteen

By the time Brandon had emptied half his bottle of beer, he was ready to leave Sully's Pub and put his plan in motion. But he couldn't bail out now. Not when he was the one who'd invited Greg to meet for a drink. So he tried to focus on what his buddy was saying.

"What this town needs is a gym," Greg said. "Don't you agree?"

"Maybe so." Brandon stayed in shape by lifting weights in his garage and running.

Greg, who stood six foot four and worked out regularly, took a chug of beer. "I'm thinking about opening one. You want to be a partner?"

"No, I don't think so." Brandon had offered to help Marissa open her business, and while she'd refused, he wanted his funds to be available in case she changed her mind. "But if you open one, I'll join."

"Okay. I've got a couple of other guys in mind."

About that time, the blonde cocktail waitress stopped by their table and offered Greg a bright-eyed smile. "Can I get you another round?"

"Sure." Greg glanced at Brandon.

He slowly shook his head. "No, thanks. Not for me."

"I'll take have another beer," Greg said. "And an order of buffalo wings."

"You got it." The blonde, who was actually quite pretty, lingered a moment longer, her gaze meeting Greg's.

When Brandon spotted a spark of mutual attraction and a flirtatious glimmer in his friend's eyes, he took the opportunity to cut out. So he got to his feet, reached into his back pocket and pulled out his wallet.

"Where are you going?" Greg asked.

"To prove myself to Marissa." Brandon glanced at the shapely, blue-eyed blonde. "Take care of my friend here."

"I sure will." She grinned from ear to ear. "My pleasure."

Brandon handed Greg a twenty to cover the

check. At least, the first round of beers and the buffalo wings.

"Good luck," Greg called to his back.

"Thanks." Brandon was going to need it.

Twenty minutes later, he arrived at Rancho Esperanza and parked in the yard. A soft light shone through the blinds in the living-room window. It was too early to turn in. Marissa must be watching TV. Or maybe she was reading.

He made his way to the front door and knocked. Moments later, she answered wearing a blue sundress, her feet bare. The sight of her took his breath away.

"Brandon," she said, her voice soft and laced with surprise.

"I hope I'm not bothering you, but we need to talk." He braced himself for the door to slam in his face, but she stepped aside instead and allowed him into the house.

That was a good sign.

He scanned the interior of the small living room—the scarred hardwood floor adorned with a blue rug, white walls sporting a fresh coat of paint and a rustic fireplace, the stones stained from smoke and soot, the mantel a rough-hewn beam.

"Have a seat," she said.

He glanced at the faded tweed recliner, then at the sofa. A bookmark peeked out of a novel that rested on the lamp table, next to where she must have been seated. He hated to push himself on her, but he hoped to have an honest, intimate conversation with her. So he bypassed the chair and chose the sofa, taking the side opposite where she'd been reading, leaving a cushion between them.

While she settled into her seat, he turned his gaze her way. Her dark hair, lush and glossy, tumbled over her shoulders, and he was tempted to touch it, to run his fingers through those curls. He waited for her to catch him looking at her, hoping she'd turn to him and smile, giving him a sign that all was right in her world.

Hell, if she could forgive her family, especially after they'd turned their backs on her when she'd needed them most, maybe that meant she'd forgive him, too. God, he sure hoped so.

"So what else did you want to talk about?" she asked.

"I told you that I trust you. And I want to prove it."

She merely studied him, looking soft and vulnerable. Yet doubtful.

"You can take Maddie and Jimmy anytime you want to have them. You can bring them here and keep them overnight—or all week. I won't even call or come by to check on them."

Her head tilted slightly. "You'd trust me with your most precious possessions?"

"Unconditionally. And if you'll let me back into your life, into your heart, you'll be just as precious to me."

She stared at him, lips parted. Soft, plump lips he'd give anything to kiss again.

"So what do you say?" he asked.

"You're serious?" she asked. "You'll let me take the kids? Unsupervised? You're not afraid I'll teach them to smoke or how to knock off a convenience store?"

He grinned. "Okay, I deserved that. Like I said, I trust you."

It would be so easy to say yes, to turn and embrace him, to thank him for giving her a chance to fit in… That is, until she recalled Betty Sue's advice.

Don't fight for *him. Fight* with *him.*

Tell him how you feel. Tell him that he'd better cut the skepticism crap when it comes to you. Stand up for yourself. Demand respect. Brandon doesn't get to make all the rules, right?

Marissa turned in her seat, her knee brushing his. She grew serious, lifted her finger and pointed it at him. "I'll consider forgiving you. But we need to get some things straight."

"I'm listening."

"Okay, then. First of all, I will *never* lie to you.

That said, you need to promise me that you will always believe me."

"No problem there. I promise."

"Secondly, I want you to forget about my record. I spent time in jail, but it was for something I didn't do. And if you don't believe me, I'll give you my stepbrother's phone number. He'll tell you those drugs were his."

"Don't need his number. I believe you, remember? We just covered that."

"All right. Then I want you to promise you'll forget about that conviction and my jail time."

"I'm afraid I can't. Not as long as you carry the pain and scars from it. That memory will be mine, too—until you're able to forget it and put it behind you."

Tears welled in her eyes, and her bravado faltered.

"Listen," he said, extending his arm to offer his hand. "Let's make a pact. Regarding our past— long past and recent past. No regrets. We won't bring it up, and we won't stew about it. No more worries. Just the here and now."

She nodded. "I like that." She shook his hand. "Agreed."

His expression turned serious. "There's one other thing. It's a big thing. Maybe. For you."

"Okay."

"I'm a deputy sheriff. I'm a good one, too. It's

what I do. And it's my career. Going forward, can you handle that?"

If he'd asked a few weeks ago, she'd have said no way. But now she realized she didn't need to run or hide anymore. This lawman was after her, and it was time to let him catch her. "Yes. I'll be honest, I'll always worry about you, but that'd be true even if you were an accountant."

"Good. Perfect." He eased closer to her on the sofa. "Is it okay if I promise something you haven't asked for?"

She nodded, shaking loose a tear that ran down her face. He reached over and wiped it away with a gentle hand. "Marissa, I promise to love you. Always. Unconditionally. And I promise to not only trust you with my kids, but with my whole heart. It's been battered in the past, first by my parents and then the twins' mother. But I can't think of entrusting it to anyone else but you."

Hope burned bright in his gaze, and any objection, any question she might have had, any condition she might have insisted upon, faded away.

"I love you, too, Brandon." Then she fell into his arms and kissed him. It began lightly at first, sweetly and with awe, then passion kicked in. She opened her mouth, and his tongue slid inside, mating with hers in a heated rush, twisting, tasting.

Her heart swelled with love for him, and her hormones spun out of control. She'd like to lead him back to her bedroom. But he had children at home, kids who needed him. Then again, maybe he had it covered.

She drew her lips from his and, resting her forehead against his, asked, "Can you stay for a while? Or do you have to go home now? I mean, are the kids okay?"

"They'll be fine until I get home."

"Good," she said. "I…um…I don't have any condoms, but for what it's worth, I'm on the pill. I was having some irregular periods, and the doctor prescribed it to straighten them out."

"And I was tested recently, when I had a department physical. All negative."

That's all she needed to know. "How long can you stay?"

"Are you inviting me for a sleepover? If so, all I have to do is make a phone call or two."

Heat rose from her toes to her nose. "I'd like nothing more than to have you spend the night."

"Then, give me a minute. I'll make that call."

After Brandon had called Mrs. Hendrix, he looked up at Marissa and winked. Then a slow smile slid across his gorgeous face.

She reached for his hand and led him down the hall and to the guest room, where she'd been staying. She'd yet to add any artwork or flowers or new bedding to make it her own, so the small, cozy room wasn't anything fancy—just a double bed, nightstand and dresser.

It certainly wasn't a honeymoon suite, even if at the moment it kind of felt like one. But Brandon wasn't a groom, and she wasn't his bride. Not yet, anyway.

But like a newlywed, she couldn't wait to make love with him, to celebrate the promises they'd made and their intentions to keep them from now on.

"This is it," she said, as they entered the room and approached the double bed covered with a blue-and-white-striped comforter.

Brandon drew her into his arms, bent his head and kissed her, slowly, thoroughly. Their mouths fit perfectly, as if they'd been made for each other. As their tongues continued to mate, their hands roamed each other's bodies, seeking, exploring, caressing.

When his fingers worked their way to her breast, his thumb skimmed across her nipple, and she whimpered. A yearning emptiness settled deep in her core. If they didn't pull back the sheets and move to the bed soon, she was going to melt into a puddle on the floor.

She slowly withdrew her lips from his, and as their gazes met, heat simmered in his eyes. He wanted her as badly as she wanted him. With a voice husky and laden with desire, she whispered,

"I want you to make love with me. Now." She turned her back to him and lifted her hair. "Will you unbutton me?"

"Gladly."

When her sundress gaped open and the cool air in the room chilled her skin, Brandon placed a kiss on her shoulders, singeing her with the warmth of his breath. She slowly turned around, removing her dress at the same time. She let it drop to the floor. Then she unhooked her bra and slipped out of it, too.

As she peeled off her panties, slowly revealing herself to him in a slow, deliberate fashion, their gazes met and locked.

"Marissa. Honey. You're more beautiful than I'd even imagined." He blessed her with a smile, then opened his arms, and she entered his embrace.

Never had she felt so loved, so cherished.

He kissed her again, and she leaned in to him, against his growing erection, and a surge of desire shot clear through her. The chemistry they shared grew stronger and even more amazing than before.

Could she ever love this man any more than she did right now?

Brandon kissed Marissa again, long and deep—savoring the taste of her, the feel of her naked body in his arms, the heat of her touch.

He slid his hands along the curve of her back and down the slope of her hips. So soft, so perfect.

He wanted her more than he'd ever wanted any other woman, and he couldn't wait to feel his bare skin against hers. He ended the kiss long enough to shuck his boots and jeans, to remove his shirt.

When they were both naked, she skimmed her nails across his chest, sending a shiver through his veins and a rush of heat through his blood. He bent and took one of her breasts in his mouth, laving the nipple, tasting her skin—the light, floral scent of her fading perfume.

He trailed kisses downward to her taut stomach, his thumbs stroking along her rib cage, as he tongued her belly button. When she let out a whimper, he raised his head and caught her eye, saw arousal written all over her pretty face.

As if on cue, she stepped back and moved to the bed, where he joined her. Then they continued to stroke, to touch, to taste until they were both nearly breathless with desire.

"I don't want to rush this," he said, as he hovered over her. "But I need to be inside you."

"There's nothing I'd like more." She reached for him, guiding his erection to where he wanted it to be.

He entered her slowly at first, but her body welcomed him with slick, liquid heat. As she arched up to meet each of his thrusts, his pace quickened.

He drove into her, in and out. She tightened her grip on his shoulders, breathing accelerated in loud gasps. She cried out as they came together in a sexual explosion that damned near took his breath away.

"I love you," he whispered. So very much. "And I love what we just did."

"Me, too. I… This was…"

When she stalled, looking for the right words, he provided them. "This was better than either of us hoped for. Did I get that right?"

She nodded. Yet neither of them moved. Brandon didn't dare. All he knew was that he wanted to hold on to her, on to this soul-stirring emotion forever.

Marissa wasn't very experienced when it came to sex, but she knew beyond a shadow of a doubt that the lovemaking she and Brandon had shared several times during the night had been incredible.

As the morning sun peered through the slats in the blinds, she rested her head on her lover's shoulder, relishing the feel of his body against hers.

"You know," Brandon said, "the twins have a birthday coming up. They're going to be five on the first of October, and I'm going to have a party for them."

"Can I help you plan it?" she asked.

"Absolutely. I hoped you would. I'm not sure how I'm going to please them both. Maddie's big on tiaras and princess gowns. And Jimmy loves superheroes."

"I'll come up with something. Don't worry."

"I don't care what it costs," he added. "But we don't need to get too fancy or carried away."

"It'll be a nice party. And lots of fun. I'll take plenty of pictures, too. I'd like to create a portfolio of parties and weddings I've planned to show future clients what they can expect from me."

"Speaking of your business plan, I've got some money put away. I mentioned it before, and you said no. But I'd really like to help you get started."

Marissa rolled to the side and braced herself on her elbow. "You won't have to help financially. I have my own money—a parting gift from my dad. He set up a trust fund for me. And that's why I went to San Diego."

Brandon turned to face her. "So that's why your stepmother and stepbrother want to make amends."

She arched a brow. "Always the cop, huh?"

"I'm sorry. I didn't mean to make you mad. I won't bring it up again. I'll trust that you know what you're doing."

A smile slid across her face. "Thanks for the vote of confidence. And just so you know, it was two hundred thousand dollars. Suzanne and I were supposed to split it equally. But she signed over her share to me. She said she was sorry she hadn't supported me through the trial or during the time I was in jail. So she wanted me to have it all."

"Wow. I wouldn't have seen that coming."

"I know. I hadn't expected that, either."

They lay there for a while, facing each other. Pondering the bond they'd created, the love they'd made.

Brandon trailed his fingers along her shoulder and down her arm. "Do you have any thoughts about that birthday party yet?"

"Don't worry. I'll have plenty of ideas. Just give me a little time. A cup of coffee should jump-start my creative process."

He chuckled. "Then, let's have breakfast, too."

"Sounds good. But what about Jimmy and Maddie? Do you need to check on them?"

"I'll call Mrs. Hendrix and tell her that we'll pick them up in an hour. Then I'll take you all to the Mulberry Café for breakfast. The kids love their pancakes."

"And I love you." Marissa brushed a kiss on Brandon's brow, then climbed out of bed. "I'll race you to the shower."

He threw off the covers and climbed out of

bed. "Is this what I can expect from now on? Fun and games?"

"Every day. For the rest of our lives."

Epilogue

It was a beautiful Saturday afternoon at Rancho Esperanza, and the twins' birthday party was in full swing. Marissa couldn't believe how well everything was going, especially considering she'd planned two separate parties and encouraged the children to all come in costume.

The adults sat at the ranch's picnic tables, and the party-rental company had brought child-size tables and chairs, along with two blow-up bouncy houses, one a castle for the girls and one a jungle gym of sorts for the boys. She'd assumed the girls would all come as a Disney princess, but one of them showed up as Princess Leia, along with a toy lightsaber. Upon arriving, they'd each hurried off to join their friends.

On the other hand, the cutest little Thor stood guard over the castle when he wasn't jumping with the princesses. It was nice to see the children intermingle like that.

"You've really outdone yourself this time," Alana said, as she approached. "Two parties in one."

Marissa turned and smiled at the woman who'd become a friend, not just a kindhearted roommate. "It's been more fun than work." She nodded at Alana's ever-expanding belly. At nearly eight months along, she would be giving birth soon. "How are you holding up?"

"Great. My feet are killing me, and my back aches. But I feel wonderful. Excited. I can't wait to have birthday parties. I never had one when I was a kid. And I've never been invited to attend one like this. It's so cool. All the parents seem to be having fun, too."

"I'd still love to plan a baby shower for you."

"Thank you, I know." Alana laughed. "I don't need one. Clay's dad has been sending daily surprises. Our little boy already has more clothes and toys than he needs. But maybe we can plan his first birthday."

"You've got a deal."

"If you'll excuse me," Alana said, "I'm going to head to the ladies' room—yet again."

Marissa laughed. "You do that. I'm going to check on the food."

As she glanced toward the house, she spotted Callie and Ramon Cruz heading toward one of the picnic tables. Ramon was pushing a twin stroller. They had the cutest little babies—a boy and a girl. And Marissa couldn't wait to see them again. Only trouble was she'd better help Ella, who'd recently returned to Rancho Esperanza after learning her abusive ex would be spending the next ten years in prison. One of the passengers in the vehicle he'd hit while driving under the influence had died.

Marissa shook her head. Such a waste and so tragic. But Ella was okay now. And healing, slowly but surely. She'd found a new home, too.

As Marissa made her way to the house, past the table where Betty Sue sat with a nice-looking man in his early seventies, with a sparkle in his blue eyes as he turned them on the older woman.

When Marissa stopped to say hello, Betty Sue beamed. "This is my friend Earl Hoffman."

She'd come with a date? You go, girl! Marissa greeted the smiling man. "It's nice to meet you. How did you two meet?"

"Playing bingo," Betty Sue said. "Earl tends bar at most of the events held at the Grange Hall. So if you ever need a bartender, he's a good one."

"That's great to know," Marissa said. "If you have a business card, I'd like it."

"Not with me." Earl nodded toward Betty Sue, their heads touching affectionately. "She'll know how to get a hold of me. Just give my gal here a ring."

Hmm. "Will do," Marissa said.

As she continued toward the house, she spotted Brandon on the back porch, talking to his friend Greg Duran. They were both tall and too handsome for their own good. But Greg was even taller, bulkier.

Marissa stopped to say hello to them, just as Greg asked Brandon, "Who's the cook? She's a cute one, but she sure jumped a mile when I said hello to her."

"Ella's not your type," Brandon said.

"What makes you think you know my type?"

"Just because." In a low voice he added, "Don't even think about asking her out." Brandon turned his focus on Marissa. "Honey, what else can I do to help?"

"I've got everything under control." She'd just turned toward the kitchen when Maddie and Jimmy came running up to her and their daddy.

"This is the bestest party ever," Jimmy said.

Maddie nodded. "I got my wish. A real castle."

"It sure looks like fun," Greg said. "And I see a big pile of presents on that table in the gazebo."

"Yeah," Jimmy said. "We can't wait to open them. But we already got the best present ever."

"Oh, yeah?" Greg asked. "What's that?"

"Daddy got us a mommy for our birthdays!" Jimmy said.

Brandon laughed. "I sure did."

"Marissa?" Maddie asked in a quiet voice. "Can we call you Mommy?"

Marissa's heart melted into a gooey mess. "Absolutely."

Maddie tugged at her brother's red cape. "Come on, Jimmy. There's Uncle Ralph and Aunt Carlene. Let's go tell them the good news. We got a mommy."

"Greg," Jimmy said, "you come, too. We want you to help us guard the castle for the girls."

"Okay, buddy," Greg said. "Always happy to help a damsel in distress."

As the kids and Greg dashed off, Brandon opened his arms, and Marissa stepped into his embrace.

"We've got a lot to celebrate," he said.

"And a lot to be thankful for." Marissa kissed the man who'd given her the world—his heart, his children and his unconditional love and trust—gifts she'd cherish forever.

* * * * *

*Don't miss the previous installments of
Rancho Esperanza,*
USA TODAY *bestselling author Judy Duarte's
new miniseries for Harlequin Special Edition:*

Callie's story
A Secret Between Us
and
Alana's story
Their Night to Remember

*Available now, wherever Harlequin books
and ebooks are sold.*

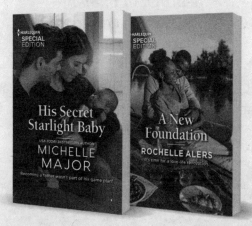

#2845 A BRAMBLEBERRY SUMMER
The Women of Brambleberry House • by RaeAnne Thayne

Rosa Galvez's attraction to Officer Wyatt Townsend is as powerful as the moon's pull on the tides. But with her past, Rosa knows better than to act on her feelings. Yet her solo life is slowly becoming a sun-filled family adventure—until dark secrets threaten to break like a summer storm.

#2846 THE RANCHER'S SUMMER SECRET
Montana Mavericks: The Real Cowboys of Bronco Heights
by Christine Rimmer

Vanessa Cruise is spending her summer working in Bronco. Rekindling her short-term fling with the hottest rancher in town? Not on her to-do list. But the handsome rancher promises to keep their relationship hidden from the town gossips, then finds himself longing for more. Convincing Vanessa he's worth the risk might be the hardest thing he's ever had to do...

#2847 THE MAJOR GETS IT RIGHT
The Camdens of Montana • by Victoria Pade

Working with Clairy McKinnon on her father's memorial tests Major Quinn Camden's every resolve! Clairy is still hurt that General McKinnon mentored Quinn over his own adoring daughter. When their years-long rivalry is replaced by undeniable attraction, Quinn wonders if the general's dying wish is the magic they both need... or if the man's secrets will tear them apart for good.

#2848 NOT THEIR FIRST RODEO
Twin Kings Ranch • by Christy Jeffries

The last thing Sheriff Marcus King needs is his past sneaking back into his present. Years ago, Violet Cortez-Hill disappeared from his life, leaving him with unanswered questions—and a lot of hurt. Now the widowed father of twins finds himself forced to interact with the pretty public defender daily. Is there still a chance to saddle up and ride off into their future?

#2849 THE NIGHT THAT CHANGED EVERYTHING
The Culhanes of Cedar River • by Helen Lacey

Winona Sheehan and Grant Culhane have been BFFs since childhood. So when Winona's sort-of-boyfriend ditches their ill-advised Vegas wedding, Grant is there. Suddenly, Winona trades one groom for another—and Grant's baby is on the way. With a years-long secret crush fulfilled, Winona wonders if her husband is ready for a family...or firmly in the friend zone.

#2850 THE SERGEANT'S MATCHMAKING DOG
Small-Town Sweethearts • by Carrie Nichols

Former Marine Gabe Bishop is focused on readjusting to civilian life. So the last thing he needs is the adorable kid next door bonding with his dog, Radar. The boy's guardian, Addie Miller, is afraid of dogs, so why does she keep coming around? Soon, Gabe finds himself becoming her shoulder to lean on. Could his new neighbors be everything Gabe never knew he needed?

**YOU CAN FIND MORE INFORMATION ON UPCOMING HARLEQUIN TITLES,
FREE EXCERPTS AND MORE AT HARLEQUIN.COM.**

HSECNM0621

*Rosa Galvez's attraction to Officer Wyatt Townsend
is as powerful as the moon's pull on the tides.
But with her past, Rosa knows better than to act on her
feelings. But her solo life slowly becomes a sun-filled,
family adventure—until dark secrets threaten to
break like a summer storm.*

*Read on for a sneak peek at
the next book in
The Women of Brambleberry House miniseries,
A Brambleberry Summer,
by* New York Times *bestselling author RaeAnne Thayne.*

"Everyone has secrets, do they not? Some they share with those they trust, some they prefer to keep to themselves."

He was quiet for a long moment. "I hope you know that if you ever want to share yours, you can trust me."

She trusted very few people. And she certainly wasn't going to trust Wyatt, who was only a temporary tenant and would be out of her life in a few short weeks.

"If I had any secrets, I might do that. But I don't. I'm a completely open book."

She tried for a breezy smile but could tell he wasn't at all convinced. In fact, he looked slightly disappointed.

She tried to ignore her guilt and opted to change the subject instead. "The lightning seems to have stopped for now. I am sure the power will be back on soon."

"No doubt."

"Thank you again for coming to my rescue. Good night. Be careful going back down the stairs."

"I will do that. Good night."

He studied her, his features unreadable in the dim light of her flashlight. He looked as if he wanted to say something else. Instead, he shook his head slightly.

"Good night."

As he turned to go back down the stairs, the masculine scent of him swirled to her. She felt that sudden wild urge to kiss him again but ignored it. Instead, she went into her darkened apartment, her dog at her heels, and firmly closed the door behind her. If only she could close the door to her thoughts as easily.

Don't miss
A Brambleberry Summer *by RaeAnne Thayne,*
available July 2021 wherever
Harlequin Special Edition books and ebooks are sold.

Harlequin.com